Colt

The Bull Riders

Maisey Yates

Chapter One

Colt

No guts, no glory, at least that's what they say.

I've always had plenty of guts, but glory in the way I want it has eluded me.

If my stepsister could hear me say that, she would punch me in the shoulder. She'd say I've had nothing but glory my entire life.

I guess that's true. In some ways. But I've never made it to the ultimate championship and won. It's the one thing that I haven't managed to get, and that makes everything feel like it doesn't matter. I'm on a mission this season to get myself back to the bull riding championships and to win.

I lost last year to my best friend, Dallas. And then he retired, which I think was kind of a dick move. Because if my win is going to count, I feel like it has to be against him, and I feel like he quit just so it never could be.

That's not really fair. He quit because he fell in love.

He quit because suddenly he found something that was more important than this.

I don't have that.

Nothing is more important to me than this.

Everyone thinks I don't care about much of anything. But they're wrong. I just don't want to scare it away by showing it my true feelings.

Because what I am is fucking intense. In a way that I know no one can really handle.

No one but the beast.

I'm standing outside the chute at the arena, looking through the slats in the metal chute at the blue merle bull. He's huge. Big, blunted horns, his snot dripping out of the front of his nose. A mean bastard.

I'm glad that I drew him.

Stone Cold. And I know that he is. That's what I need. A killer.

I need a killer, because I need a good ride. Hell, it's not enough to be good, it's got to be a bang. At this level, it's not enough to just stay on for eight seconds.

"Are you going to give me a good show?" I ask, tapping my fist against the chute, getting a reaction out of the bull, who kicks at the side of it.

"Yeah, buddy."

I climb up the side of the chute and sit on the top, waiting for the right moment to get on the bull's back.

I get a signal from the gate attendant and get down over the top of him. He jerks underneath me, and I tighten the strap around my hand, adjusting everything, getting a feel for where I'm sitting. I can feel him breathing underneath my thighs.

"All right," I say. "We are one, buddy." I lean down and pat the bull on his shoulders and feel them twitch beneath my palm. Hot and revved up, ready to go. "We're doing this together. You and me. We're taking this all the way to the championship."

He kicks the side of the chute aggressively, and I pat him again.

"Twenty-five years old, here in Central Point all the way from Gold Valley, Oregon, folks, over one million dollars in winnings, been to the championships three years in a row, it's Colt Campbell."

The music starts, and I know the gate is about to open. I grab on as tightly as I can, nod at the gate attendant, and it bursts open. The bull is all energy. Lightning and thunder as we rumble out into the arena. I maneuver and try to get my body into the best position to find my groove, but I can't quite seem to get it.

He's bucking, rolling, and then I realize he's moving right toward the wall.

Fuck, if that bastard smashes me up against the cement...

But then he moves in an entirely different direction, and I find myself flying through the air. It's been so long since I've been bucked off, I can't accept what's happening even as I'm sailing down toward the ground.

But I don't hit.

Not the arena dirt, anyway.

All of a sudden, there's a sharp pain in my ribs, and I realize the fucking worst has happened. Stone Cold whips his head underneath me, catches me, and flips me back up into the air.

Then, as I'm coming down again, he lowers his head, grinding my midsection down into the arena dirt as I hit. This isn't a benign shaking off of the rider. This is intentional destruction.

He comes down on me as he lowers his head and rakes his horns against me again. I feel something hot and wet on my face. For some reason, I think it must be bull snot until I put my hand there and it comes away dark red, and I realize this motherfucker is tearing me to pieces.

I look up into the stands just for one second, as he continues to ravage me.

I'm getting killed in front of my family.

My guts are about to be all over the arena. With no glory to be had.

Chapter Two

Allison

I'm screaming. Screaming and screaming. I'm watching from the stands while Colt Campbell dies.

There's a feeling inside me, persistent and horrible, like a piece of myself is being torn away from my body with every pass the bull makes over Colt's ragdoll frame.

Which makes no sense, but it's a sensation so strong I'm almost overwhelmed by it.

Nobody seems to be able to get the bull away from him.

The bullfighters are doing everything they can, and men on horseback have the bull lassoed by the horns now, trying to at least draw some of that animal's fire back onto them.

Finally, they have the bull bound up enough that he can't keep going back in on Colt. The crowd is in a frenzy, and the woman next to me collapses against the man she's sitting next to. I think she might actually be unconscious.

The announcer is saying something about ambulances, about emergencies and protocols, but his words fade out into an indistinct buzzing. I can't process language anymore. All I see is Colt. Lying there, broken. Completely ravaged by that animal.

I don't *like* Colt, but I'm a human, and so is he. I would feel devastated watching this happen to anyone. Plus, he's my stepbrother, and I love his mom. Cindy has been so good to me for so many years, and

His mom, my stepmom, ran out of the stands with my dad, and I'm just there, frozen. Gentry, my brother, is sitting beside me, holding onto my shoulders. "Are you okay?"

"No." I'm not. There's a pit in my stomach I can't imagine ever going away. I don't know what to do next. I'm frozen.

Gentry tugs on my arm. "Let's go. We'll figure out where they took him. I assume Dad and Cindy went there. Then we can get to the hospital. Cindy will probably go in the ambulance with him."

I look back at the arena. At the dirt, dark, and wet with his blood.

I don't know how a person can bleed that much and not have bled their whole soul out.

"Do you think he's alive, Gentry?" My lips are numb as I ask the question.

He stares ahead, his face waxen. "I don't know, Sprite."

I've never seen my brother look like this. Like he might throw up, or like he might cry. He and Colt are so close. Best friends, honestly. They have been since before our parents married each other. They kind of parent-trapped them, honestly. It was the best thing that ever happened to Gentry. The worst thing that ever happened to me, for reasons that I've never wanted to talk about.

But as difficult as my relationship is with Colt, seeing him hurt like that...

I'm floating above myself. Now that I'm done screaming, my whole body feels like it's a husk. I'm dimly aware that we've stood up and are walking out of the stands, headed toward the medical triage center that was set up, because even though this so rarely happens, it can.

By and large, it's usually people, attendees of the rodeo, getting treated for heatstroke, or getting bandaged up after some fistfight has erupted.

It's rarely the riders. But when it is, it can be serious. Deadly.

I've always known that in theory. That what he does is dangerous.

Now it feels far too real.

We get to the tent, and I see him on a gurney, right in front of the ambulance. They've got a bandage over his head, stopping some of the bleeding, his midsection packed with gauze. They have his leg in a splint.

He's not conscious. Not moving.

I'm not even sure what to be most worried about. The wound in his midsection, his clearly shattered leg, or his head injury. That bull went horn to forehead with Colt, and I know that...

He has a mask and a helmet that he wears. And I'm so grateful for that, because without it, I know he would be dead. I know that it stopped the full force of what happened, but him bleeding like that, just because the bull clipped him right under the helmet, shows how devastating that would've been without it.

His mother loads up into the ambulance with him, and I meet eyes with her, her face tear-streaked. I want to do something, say something, but I don't know how to speak anymore. I don't know what to say. I don't feel like I can really say anything. Everything just feels like a blur. A horrendous, awful blur.

My dad scrubs his hand over his face. "Allison, would you... Would you please drive his truck to the hospital?"

He reaches into his pocket and takes out a set of keys. "He always gives them to me before the ride." I've never seen my dad look like this before. He looks like he's going to keel over.

"Yeah. I will."

"I don't know if I can drive. I feel like I'm going to throw up. But I don't want to do it in front of my dad. I don't want to do it in front of Gentry.

"Do you know where it is?"

"I think so," I say.

He parks in the lot designated for the cowboys, and it's the most garish red truck you've ever seen, with oversized tires. It's easy to find.

I clutch the key fob in my hand, and I walk away. As soon as I round the corner to where the cowboys park, I scurry quickly over to a planter box, and I vomit. I retch until there's nothing left in my stomach. Until I'm dry heaving. Then I straighten back up and wipe my mouth. This is *awful.*

My heart feels like it's being torn into pieces.

You would think that I was still in love with him.

But I know better than that. I thought I knew what being in love was when I was thirteen, and he was sixteen, glorious, and my brother's best friend. The Golden Boy of Gold Valley. The most popular, unattainable figure in town.

The best and the brightest.

When our parents married each other, I cried and cried. I made myself sick the night before the wedding. Kind of like I was just sick right now. I wonder how many times I've vomited over Colt Campbell. That's kind of an ignominious honor.

Not that he'll ever know. I'll never, ever tell him. It would have to be tortured out of me. Because I can think of nothing worse than having to admit having feelings for him. It's so basic, honestly. Every girl had a crush on him, but I actually knew him. I know him still. Not that we can ever be in the same room without sniping at each other.

My fault, admittedly. But it's a survival technique.

I had to distance myself from him after he moved into my house. Could there be anything more mortifying for a thirteen-year-old girl in love? To have the object of your affection move into your house? Having him see you at your absolute worst. With acne, in the morning, while PMS-ing. It was an actual nightmare. I couldn't see another option besides putting myself in the bratty sister category.

And if the physical attraction to him hasn't worn off entirely, that's just because he's hot. Tragically hot, if I'm honest.

But that doesn't mean I want him.

I stop right outside of his truck, and I unlock the doors.

He might not make it. A tear slides down my cheek that I didn't even realize was there, and I reach up to wipe it away.

Colt.

Fuck.

I bite the inside of my cheek and try to pull it together. My dad asked me to drive the truck to the hospital, and I need to do that. I need to do this one simple thing that he asked me to do. I can do it. I can do it.

I take a deep breath, and I open up the driver's side of the truck. I get inside. With shaking hands, I push the ignition button, and then I realize that I don't know which hospital we're going to. There are two in Medford, and I don't know which one.

I call Gentry, who's on his way there in his truck. I rode over with him. "Which one?"

He tells me, and I put the directions in on my phone. Gentry and I stay on the phone, silent as we both drive in our separate vehicles. When we get there, everything is chaos. We can't see him, because he's been rushed straight to surgery.

He's not conscious.

Not conscious.

I can't bear the thought of it. He's twenty-five years old. I can't bear the idea that the most fraught, complicated relationship of my life might just be over. With no resolution, no gain, no... Nothing.

I can't fathom that a bright spark like Colt Campbell might be snuffed out forever.

Chapter Three

Colt

I wake up *violent*. The air rushes into my lungs like a shock. I gasp, trying to sit up in a hospital bed that won't let me move. "The fuck," I shout.

Everything hurts like a son of a bitch from my head on down. It's like I'm made of pain.

"Colt! Oh my God."

I look to my left and see my mother staring at me, her face pale and streaked with tears. She rushes over to the bedside and begins to push a button next to my hand. Over and over again. "I have to call the nurse." She's shaking, visibly upset, and I can't stand to be the reason my mom is crying.

Everything feels turned around in my head. I'm in a hospital but I don't know why. My mom is here and that makes me feel – for a second – like maybe I'm here to see her but...

No. Everything hurts. So it's not her who's admitted to the hospital.

And then I remember, because suddenly I feel my body. Really feel it. *Shit.*

I know what happened...

Yes, I do.

It all comes back. Getting ground into the dust. Torn asunder, actually.

It's a fucking miracle that I'm awake. Unless I'm dead, and this is my version of hell.

My mom crying while I'm bed bound and hooked up to wires, needles and beeping machinery.

I wiggle my fingers, my toes, and they move. I also don't see any imps or demons hopping around the room so maybe I'm not dead.

My fingers and toes work, so that's good to know.

I don't know what my injuries are, though. I don't know...

"What day is it?"

"Friday," my mom says.

The last thing I remember is Saturday night at the rodeo. So either I went back in time or it's been nearly a week.

"I've been out that long?"

"Yes. They were keeping you sedated to watch for swelling in your brain, and you've been heavily dosed with meds."

"*This* is heavily dosed?" My entire body feels like it got dragged to hell by a freight train. If this is what it's like on pain meds, I don't want to have anything to do with them.

I let my head fall back for a moment, then turn toward the door.

And I see her. Like an angel. Of death, most likely. Standing there with the light shining on her red hair.

My gorgeous, bratty stepsister.

What a pain in my ass that girl is.

Has been for years. Especially around the time I started to notice she was beautiful. Luckily, she hates me. That makes things easier.

Though it's not *hate* that I see on her face right now. It's worry. So, I guess she doesn't hate me so much that she wishes me into an early grave. Which is something, I suppose, even if it is a small thing.

"You're awake," she says.

"Reluctantly."

Then, a medical team comes in. My room is like a clown car of doctors. Everyone's looking at readouts and vitals. And then there's a doctor who comes in to talk to me about recovery.

I'm lucky, I didn't get a severe head injury – I'm told. It was bad enough. I had a concussion; if I hadn't had the helmet on, my whole head would've caved in. There's absolutely no question about that. But the superficial wounds on my head were the worst part. The bull managed to graze me with that horn underneath the front grate on the helmet, and he tore my scalp from the center of my forehead down toward my ear.

I've got a fuckton of stitches there.

The real issue is scar tissue that could develop in my torso. He tore open my midsection, and there was apparently a substantial amount of repair that had to be done internally. They said it's the kind of surgical scarring prone to creating networks of stubborn, healed-over scars, making movement stiff. Then there's the issue of my leg. The description of my leg injury is actually so graphic that I almost feel a little bit sick. I look up at my mom, who I realize saw it all

"We had to go into the arena later that night and look for your bones," she whispers.

Fuck.

My thigh busted open, and I lost bone in my femur. The doctor says it has the potential to be a life-changing injury. I'm lucky I didn't lose it. The operation involved them methodically piecing my shattered bone back together, and it's possible there will be long-term chronic pain and reduced mobility.

No. I just don't accept that. I won't accept it. I don't want to."

"It's a very long healing process. You won't be putting weight on this leg for four to six months." The doctor looks at me, his grey eyes steady on mine. "I know that is not going to be a pleasant process. But I've gotten to know your family over the last few days, and everyone says that you're strong and you're stubborn. So, you're going to do your PT and do the best you can. You're not going to give up."

Being in the kind of pain I'm in, knowing that I'm essentially one giant stitched-up bag of cracked loose bones, makes me *want* to give up before I even have to start. This kind of helplessness is something I've never experienced before. I want to escape my body.

This is some bullshit, honestly.

I've got a cast from the top of my thigh down to my toes. I can't move at all.

"But the championship is in October."

"You're not going to the championship," my mom says, her voice firm. "Even if you healed, you didn't get any points for that ride."

I grit my teeth together, and I know she's saying that

because she doesn't want me to hope. Because I would have to keep competing if I wanted to go to the championship, since that ride fucked me all up, and while I might be crazy enough to try and get myself healed by October, I know that I won't be healed in time for any of the rides leading up to that.

"But..."

I feel like a child. Sitting there arguing against logic and medical authority. But it just doesn't seem... Like the kind of thing that could possibly happen to me. I've been working at this for so long. I'm good. I've never had an injury that came anywhere close to this, and Dallas Dodge and I have been riding bulls since we were sixteen.

I look around the room for the first time, past my family. It's an explosion of balloons and flowers. Sent from...I wonder who all sent all this?

"Has Dallas been here?" I ask.

"Of course," my mom says. "He was here earlier today."

I frown. It's a long drive from Medford to Gold Valley.

Then I look out the window.

"Where are we?"

"They moved you to Tolowa Medical Center."

I have no memory of a move. At all. The last six days are just...gone for me. Gone forever.

"Right."

Gentry and his dad come into the room next. "This is what happens when we go pick up dinner," Jim says, holding up a takeout box.

"Don't worry about it," I say to him. I'm lucky.

My stepdad is a good guy. Before him, there was no father figure in my life at all. My own dad fucked off before I was born, and my mom was a single mom most of my life, working as hard as she could, establishing a successful real estate business before she got into buying and renting out houses. Allison and Gentry's mom died of cancer when they were little. Gentry and I hatched a brilliant plan to hook our parents up, and it really worked. The rest is history, and we're almost one big happy family.

Except for Allison hating me.

"Can I get some of that food?"

"We have to check with your doctor," my mom says as my family all sits down at a table across the room and starts to dig into the takeout. It feels mean.

I'm a bit comforted by the meanness, if I'm honest. Because at least I know I'm not dying. If they were all being too nice, then I would think that the doctors were lying, and I had some kind of ticking time bomb injury that was going to result in my untimely demise.

Especially if Allison started being nice.

I'm out of it, even though I'm awake now. Drifting in and out of consciousness as I lie there in bed, unable to stay fully awake, but I know my family is all there.

Not all of them.

Images of my dad— my biological dad— click through in my head like a slideshow. Because I only have a few memories of him. Very specific, and very short. In his cowboy hat, his Wrangler jeans, his boots, walking away from me at a rodeo. I had just done the mutton busting and fallen on my ass.

Did you see, Dad?

I don't know if he saw. I don't remember. I was little. It doesn't really matter.

And then again, at my... It was a birthday. But it wasn't my party. We met at the zoo.

I can still see him standing, facing away from me.

Watch this!

I wake up with a start. It's dark. And I can't see anything.

There's a faint shape in the corner, in the chair. And I remember where I am. The hospital. When I went to sleep, my family was eating dinner, and now they're gone.

But *someone's* there.

"Hello?"

I hear groggy, sleepy sounds, and I realize that whoever's there they were snoozing pretty hard.

"Do you need something?"

Allison. Allison is still here.

"What are you doing here?" I ask.

She makes an exasperated sound, and I see as she rises up into a standing position, looking more like a ghost than a person in the dimly lit room.

"Your mom needed to sleep. To actually sleep through the night. And now that you aren't on death's door..."

"Was I on death's door?"

I can see her crossing her arms even through the darkness.

"It looks like it for a while. Before they moved you. You were stabilized by the time they flew you here from Medford."

"They flew me here? And I missed it?"

"Yeah. You have a head injury." She moves toward me, standing at the foot of the bed. "And, not only did you have a head injury, you were on enough painkillers to put that bull down."

"I've heard that," I say, then, "*Did* they put the bull down?" I realize that I'll be unhappy if so. Because a bull doesn't choose to be ridden, but I chose to ride. And whatever happens as a result, the consequences are on the cowboy. The animal shouldn't bear any.

"I know."

"Well, I want to find out. And tell them not to."

"He wanted to kill *you*."

"Yeah, I know, but that doesn't mean I want him to die."

She puts her hands on the footboard of the hospital bed and leans in. "It doesn't make any sense that you would want to defend the animal that tried to kill you."

"Maybe it doesn't. Maybe it doesn't make any sense. But it's how I feel. I put myself in that situation. I took the risk. And I'm going to do it again."

"Are you out of your mind?"

"No. I'm not out of my mind. But this isn't me." I gesture around the hospital room. "This is my life. I'm not going to be in here forever. I'm going to go back on the circuit. I still haven't won a championship yet. I've got winning to do."

"Colt," she says, like she's talking to a child, patronizing and lowering. "You aren't just going to bounce back from this."

"I'm going to be the best god damn patient that anyone has ever seen," I say, frustration bubbling up inside of me. "The doctor is just talking about averages. Bone grafts and shit. I think I feel better already."

"*You* are on *morphine*. And you don't know how you feel."

"Being in nursing school doesn't make you an expert."

"Being *you* doesn't make you an expert," she says. "Whatever you may like to think. You don't know better than your doctors, you dumbass."

"I didn't say I did. I am saying that I'm going to do a hell of a lot better than average. I'm going to get back on the bull."

She makes an exasperated sound. "I'm not arguing with you at three in the morning."

I look around and suddenly realize where I am, yet again. I keep losing myself. My brain feels fuzzy, and I'm not sure why. Morphine. She said that.

But I've never not been able to will my way out of a situation that I didn't like. It just seems like, because I'm awake, my brain should be working the way I want it to. And because I want to get back into the rodeo, my body should obey. It always has. It's always been like that for me.

"You need to take the time to recover," she says. "If you don't do that, you're not going to be able to do anything."

I look away from her. When I roll my head back over, she's standing right next to me. It startles me. I can't remember the last time Allison got anywhere near me of her own free will.

"Colt," she says, her eyes sincere in the darkness. "That was the most horrendous thing I've ever seen in my entire life. You probably don't remember it, but I will, for the rest of my life. When your mom came back to the hospital with your bones..." Her breath catches. "We all know what you just went through. You don't. So maybe you should shut up, and quit being so arrogant and listen to other people for once in your God damned life."

She goes away from the bed, back to the corner. She sits in the chair, and I get the impression that she's done with me for the night.

Then I fall back into an uneasy sleep. Filled with strange and disturbing dreams. About death. Dying.

Being crushed beneath the weight of the bull, my dad is looking away from me.

Did you see?

He never turns around.

Chapter Four

Allison

When I wake up the next morning, I feel dizzy and a bit disoriented. I blame the interrupted sleep I got last night, not that sleeping in the hospital room is all that comfortable to begin with.

It's why Cindy needed to take a break.

There's a window seat bed in the hospital, but there's something about it that I couldn't get used to, so I ended up just sitting in the recliner.

Still, I'm out of sorts, which is just a testament to this whole thing. It's been a week from hell. And of course, now that Colt is awake, it's not like he's making things any easier. I can't really be mad at him about last night.

He was borderline hallucinating, I'm sure.

Between the morphine and how out of it and exhausted he has to be just from his body trying to heal these injuries, there's no way he can be held accountable for his nonsense.

I'm just glad that there's a team of doctors taking care of

him. And not me. He's guaranteed to be the worst patient alive. This is maybe the only time that I'm glad I'm not quite done with nursing school.

Being in the hospital, though, is giving me a window into the way my life is going to look when I start clinical rotations. When I graduate.

It still seems far away now, but I guess it's not really.

I stand up and I look at him. There's no one here. I haven't been alone with him other than last night and now. I take the moment to just look. He's hooked up to all manner of wires, his leg in traction. He seems totally out.

He's still got an oxygen tube just below his nostrils, his face still a little swollen. There's so much bruising around his stitches, one artful contusion and an abrasion on his high cheekbone. The kind of injury they would put on the hero in an action movie. The rest of his injuries, though, are less aesthetic. I know that his midsection was pretty severely gored, and even though he didn't sustain any injuries to his internal organs, his skin was torn open through the muscle in parts.

Right now, his leg is the big concern as far as long term effects. But being gored had to have been so...awful.

I suddenly feel lightheaded, thinking about all of his injuries. All the pain that he must be in.

I decide that I need to go get some breakfast. I wander down to the cafeteria and get in line. For some reason, scenes of his accident keep playing in my mind, over and over again.

Him getting thrown off and landing on the ground. The bull going after him. Slashing him.

I blink, trying to wipe my mind clean of the image, and then keep walking forward. I take a carton of milk out of the fridge, and I'm about to go over and grab an apple from the fruit bowl when I start to feel woozy. By the time I see black spots in front of my eyes, it's too late. My stomach cramps unbearably. I feel so sick, like I'm going to...

Not vomit.

It almost feels like I'm dying.

Then, my knees lock and I fall. Forward. I hit my head on the corner of the counter and fall backward onto the floor as I lose consciousness. I'm out, then back. The blackness recedes, and I lie there, the back of my neck sweaty, my body hot and cold at the same time.

Hospital staff are converging on me. Then, someone is shining a light in my eyes and checking my vitals.

"I'm okay," I say. "I passed out."

"You hit your head," one of the women hovering above me says.

"Oh." I touch my forehead. It hurts. Yes. I did hit my head. I know that. I know that I hit my head.

"I think you have a concussion," the nurse says, shining a light in my eyes.

I try to turn away from the blinding sight. "Oh."

They help me sit up slowly. And then I'm the one getting taken into triage, getting examined.

"You know what caused you to pass out?"

"I just think it was because I hadn't eaten," I say. I admit that it's probably from imagining Colt's accident. Thinking about it again makes my stomach cramp up. I don't know why it's affecting me like this. It's ridiculous. It's definitely not because of some crush I had on him when I was thirteen. I know it has something to do with the violent nature of all of it, but I've been watching videos. I've been working toward being able to be in emergency room-type situations, and I'm supposed to be... Able to handle this. I'm supposed to know what I'm doing. I'm supposed to be good at it.

"I'm a nursing student," I say.

"Well, we definitely need more nurses," the nurse says to me.

"I know," I say.

My words are bland, kind of stupid. I wish that I could say something a little bit more intelligent.

"You shouldn't be alone tonight."

"I'm staying in the hospital. My... My stepbrother is here. He's the rodeo rider who got hurt."

"Oh," she says. "Right. He's in a bad way."

"Yeah," I say. "That's not why I passed out. I can handle this. It's just... I should have eaten sooner."

"Do you often pass out when you don't eat?"

"No."

"It's okay that seeing a family member hurt like this upset you." She's looking at me compassionately. But for some reason, that just frustrates me.

"No. He's okay. It's not that. But anyway, I'm going to be here tonight, so I'll be observed. I'm not going to die in my sleep."

"That's good to know," she says.

"Yeah," I say. "Good to know."

I get up, like I'm going to walk out. "No," she says. "Let's get you a wheelchair, and I'll take you up to his room, and then I can bring you some food. Since apparently that's what you need to function."

What I need is for my stepbrother not to be broken up and near death in a hospital room, but I decide not to say that. The churning in my stomach makes it hard for me to deny that everything happening with Colt isn't part of this. Maybe I'm not weak when it comes to medical stuff. Maybe it's just him.

I don't really think I like that any better. But it doesn't

matter if I like it or not, because here I am, getting wheeled back to his room.

Maybe he'll be asleep. He's pretty hopped up on morphine, so it's possible that he won't react when I get brought in.

I get wheeled through the open door, and Colt lifts his head, his eyes meeting mine the minute I cross the threshold into the room.

No such luck as going undetected, I fear.

"What the hell happened to you?"

"I'm fine," I say.

I stand up, and move on unsteady legs over to the chair. I'm a little bit shakier than I realized.

"Okay. You don't look fine, but also, that doesn't answer my question."

"Your food will be up soon," the nurse says to me, and I nod, sitting back in the chair and fixing my gaze on the back wall.

"Allison," he says, his tone cajoling.

"You're injured," I say. "Shouldn't you be lying there in pain and self-pity?"

"I don't know that you want me to sink into the swamp of my own self-pity. It's unattractive. Honestly, it would be embarrassing for both of us."

I look at him, his strong athletic body completely bound up in the bed. Self-pity is coming. I can feel it. Because he's going to want things to be a certain way, and he's going to have to wait for the actual healing process to take effect. I don't think that Colt Campbell has ever, ever thought that he was subject to the laws that every other man had to endure. He's always moved through the world as if a light shines upon him. Down from the heavens. One that gifts him with incredible talent to do whatever he wants, to be liked by everyone. Social anxiety is afraid of Colt, not the other way around.

And I just have a feeling that when he really contends with the reality that he isn't going to just be able to rise out of bed and walk on command, he's going to be very, very unhappy.

"I passed out," I admit. Because the longer that I spin this out, the weirder it's going to be.

"What?"

"I passed out in the cafeteria, and I hit my head." I indicate the bump on my forehead, which I can feel growing as each moment passes.

"Jesus Christ, Allison."

"*What?* You're saying that like I *chose* to do it, like I'm stealing your thunder. I'm not your little sister on that level." Those words come out in a rush, and I regret them when he looks at me with a light in his eyes that makes my stomach go tight.

"You kind of *are*," he says, his tone dry. "I mean, here I am, the victim of a hideous accident, and you have to go get yourself admitted to the hospital too?"

"I'm *not* admitted," I clarify. "It's not that bad. I'm just safer if I'm not alone, and hey, I'm not, because I'm staying with you so that your mom can have a break."

"I'm not a toddler. I'm not going to wander out of here if I'm left unsupervised."

We glance at each other, and I fight the urge to smile, because there is a small amount of humor in that. As terrible as it all is.

"If you weren't in traction, you might, though, and we both know that."

"True. Are you okay?"

The sincere concern in his tone warms me. It's rare that

Colt and I have an exchange that could be called anything like sincere. I'm not really sure if it's his fault or mine. Or if it's just a pattern that we're in. One that we've created over years, where I'm kind of a brat to him, and he teases me, which makes me angry, because I don't want him to tease me.

That's all old stuff. I remember hating it, because it felt like he was making me into that little sister that I never wanted to be to him. It's complicated, because I really do love his mom. She's been wonderful. She brought a substantial amount of joy into our family, and into my dad's life specifically. After my mom died, it was like a piece of him was missing. Cindy brought a different piece into his life. Not the same one that went away when my mom died, but something entirely new.

Something he very much deserved.

But having to deal with the indignity of my painful secret crush becoming my stepbrother almost killed me.

Okay, it didn't almost kill me, but I was thirteen, so it felt about as fatal as anything can.

It still doesn't feel great.

And our foundation is built on that crunchy, difficult, awful time.

He probably doesn't even know why. And if I were really mature, maybe I would let my guard down and talk to him about it with some honesty. Because it isn't like I...

Our eyes meet, I catch my breath, and look away.

No. It's not like that. But it doesn't mean I don't know how beautiful he is. Even as messed up as he is right now.

"You need to take care of yourself," he says.

"I'm taking care of myself," I say, trying to keep the attitude out of my voice.

Someone in scrubs comes in with a cart laden with food, leaves a tray next to Colt, and then one next to me.

"Thank you," I say, as I lift the lid on the tray, and am greeted by food that looks shockingly decent.

"I just have... I got lightheaded, because I haven't eaten," I say, indicating the plate of food in front of me.

"Well, you ought to eat," he says.

"Yes. That's what I'm doing."

He looks over at the tray. "I'm not that hungry."

"Probably because you've been on an IV drip. It's very likely that you're swollen with fluids."

"Well," Colt says. "Just when I thought I couldn't feel any sexier, not only is my leg up in traction, and my head is stitched back together, and I think I have gauze packed into my stomach, but I'm swollen with fluids. Truly, this is a high point."

I pause, my fork midway between the plate and my mouth. I don't want to tell him that he's sexy. The problem is, he *is* sexy. It doesn't matter that he's bedbound. Doesn't matter that he's hurt. Or that he might be full of fluids. He's an attractive man. He exudes it. In a way that is theoretical to me, and not specifically personal. He's just aesthetically, and arguably handsome, and on top of that he's got that charisma that makes people stop and look at him no matter what they're doing.

"Somehow, I have a feeling you'll have seduced a hospital employee before you get out of here."

He barks a laugh, and my heart clenches tight. It's the closest thing to a compliment I could give him without making it personal to me, or what I think of him. But now I'm forced to imagine him gripping a nurse by the hips and pulling her into bed and –

Nope. Don't like that. I hate it. Thanks. No more imagining Colt getting it on with somebody whilst still bound to his hospital bed. Because if anyone could. He could. And I find that bothersome. Even if I shouldn't. Well, I know I shouldn't. I should be all for him getting his healing no matter how he finds it. Sexual healing included. But it feels gross, and I don't like it.

"I don't know that I feel inclined toward seduction at the moment," he says.

"Well, you deserve it," I say. "As a little treat."

"I would like to go back in time as a little treat and not be dealing with this." He lets his head fall back on the pillow, a rueful expression on his face. "Sorry. That probably is the morphine talking. Self-pity really isn't my jam, normally."

"I think you're allowed to have a little bit of self-pity," I say.

My chest feels tight. This whole thing has just been... Awful. Terrible.

"I guess I'm going to be home for a while."

His voice is rough now.

"Yeah."

"We'll be neighbors again."

I rent a house from my mom in town, where I work at a jewelry store, while going to school for nursing. Colt lives two doors down from me, but generally, he's not there. It's essentially where he keeps his stuff. I know that eventually, he plans on buying a ranch. When he settles down and has time to run it. At the moment, competing in the rodeo, he's gone too much. He helps my dad with his ranch, but he won't even be able to do that.

My throat gets tight all over again. My emotions are decidedly all over the place, and I need to get a grip. Colt is the one who's injured. He's the one who's entitled to difficult feelings. I need to get over myself.

"Yeah. Well. Once you get out of here." That wasn't all that encouraging. "Sorry. Hopefully it won't be very long. I mean... You're stable now."

He laughs. "Stable. Yeah. I feel really stable."

"Colt..."

"It's fine. It's fine. Because... There are all kinds of things in life you don't choose. But you have to live with them anyway. Right?"

I feel like he's actually asking me.

"Well. Yes."

I don't feel like I'm the right person to give him insight into anything.

"So, I just have to deal with this."

"Yeah." I bite the inside of my cheek. "You get to be mad about it."

He seems to think about that for a long moment. "Not so mad I throw myself on the ground and get a concussion."

I give him a hard stare. "You already had one of those."

"Did you just want to match me? You could have just bought us bracelets. A friendship-concussion is a little over the top."

"We're not friends."

Instantly, I regret it. I regret that those words came out of my mouth. I regret that they were so ready, there on the tip of my tongue, that insane self-defense that I always have to do when I feel like I'm getting too close to him. Like I'm a scared, solo traveler in a hotel room, desperately piling up furniture in front of the door to keep it from being opened.

There's a door with Colt that I really want to keep closed. That I need to keep closed.

But still, I don't need to be a bitch like that.

"Because we're family." Those words feel dragged out of the center of my throat. I don't especially want to be family to that man. I never have. I can't leave that clunky, awful sentence lingering in the air between us. Because it's just terrible. It's just way too mean.

"Yeah," he says.

He's spacing out a little bit, which is actually good. His morphine drip must have given him another dose. And I don't need to keep talking. I don't need to keep trying to dig myself out of this pit. In fact, what I really need is to just let it all go. I need to rest, because I also have a head injury.

Of all the stupid things.

Maybe that's why I said that. Maybe it wasn't me just being desperate. Maybe it wasn't actually about all my complicated feelings that I shouldn't have for my stepbrother.

But as he drifts off to sleep, and I look at the expression on his face, I worry very much that it's exactly that.

Chapter Five

Colt

The first thing I remember when I wake up is that Allison got a concussion. My eyes open, and I look around the hospital room, which is empty.

Instantly, I'm worried that something worse happened to her. That her condition deteriorated, or something.

If her brain turns to jelly because I had a bull riding accident that's really going to affect the family holidays. Plus, I'll feel guilty. I've never really felt guilty before, and I don't think it would be a good look for me.

I'm joking in my own mind for about thirty seconds before I actually start getting scared something is wrong with her. I'm examining all the lines I'm hooked up to and trying to decide if I can make an escape when she appears in the doorway.

"What are you doing?" she asks.

I'm holding onto my IV pole, and I guess I look like I'm

about to unplug from everything – which I was absolutely about to do.

"Nothing." I relax back into the bed.

"I was just grabbing a snack and seeing if I'm feeling okay."

"Well. I thought you died."

She wrinkles her nose. "No, you didn't."

"I thought something happened."

Her brows knit together, and she's staring at me like she doesn't know what to do with me. Fair enough, in this hospital bed hooked up to all this shit I don't even know what to do with me.

"I don't really need you to worry about me. Considering I'm not the one who just about got torn to pieces in front of an audience."

I grimace. "Don't downgrade me. I was *torn to pieces.*" I wave my hand up and down over my midsection. "I'm stitched back together."

She looks at me with a measure of something that might actually be compassion. Hard to imagine on Allison, if I'm honest.

The moment between us is broken by the arrival of my mom and Jim.

"I hear they're going to try and help you stand today," my mom says upon entry.

"News to me," I say.

But I'm ready for that. I'm tired of being in this bed. Hell, I'm tired of being in the hospital. I can't do anything. I feel helpless, and I hate that. My ass is rotting as I sit here, melding into one flesh with the hospital bed.

The worst thought ever, and I hate myself for having it.

I'm ready to get moving. I'm ready to get out of here.

"Did you know that Allison got a concussion?" I don't

know why I say that. Except I'm tired of everybody looking at me like I'm an object of pity, and it felt like it might be nice to spread some of that around. Though I can feel flames burning into the side of my face from the intensity of her gaze. I don't even have to look at her to know that she's wishing I had met a painful end in that arena.

"What?" Jim is immediately crossing the room and moving toward her, and my mom isn't far behind.

"I'm fine," she says. "I fainted in the cafeteria yesterday. It's not a big deal. They didn't even admit me."

"Why didn't you call?" Jim asks.

"Because I didn't need anything. They just didn't want me to go back home and sleep in the apartment by myself. But I'm here, in a hospital. There isn't a safer place to be."

I can tell that she's ready to throttle me, but I'm kind of enjoying it. I don't need to be the bearer of everyone's concern. But it's ridiculous, and I hate it.

"It's not a big deal, and he's just trying to deflect."

"Well, I hate to hog all the attention."

She gives me a murderous glare, and then stalks from the room, Jim on her heels.

"She's so difficult." I make a very sympathetic face at my mother, as if I can only offer my condolences for how much of a pain her stepdaughter is.

My mom is staring down at me, and I can see that she's not amused by the fact that Allison and I are having conflict. But honestly, what else is new?

Allison and I are oil and water. Have been, will be, always.

"You should've texted me about her," Mom says.

"Sorry. I was busy being wounded."

Mom rolls her eyes upward, like she's annoyed at God

for giving her all of us kids. "I don't know what to do with any of you."

"Gentry is fine," I say.

"He's out on a fire," she says. "Which is the one reason he's not here. And I have to worry about him the whole time he's doing that. I didn't think I had to worry about Allison."

"Yeah, out of the three of us, she's definitely the one least likely to encounter a workplace injury."

Of course, I may never actually do my work ever again. It might be over. I might be over. Done. Finished. Who can say? I can't take that on board. I never won. Not *everything*. Not like Dallas, who won the championship last year, and I was sure... I was sure that this was my year. It's probably going to be Maverick Quinn, which makes me want to commit a murder, because that guy is a prick of the highest order, and I don't have any patience for his bullshit, much less him winning anything.

And I definitely didn't aim to retire at twenty-five, with so much left to do. It makes my gut churn with rage. That feeling of being out of control. That feeling of helplessness. That maybe wanting something isn't enough to make it happen. That working as hard as I fucking can isn't going to be sufficient here.

It's bullshit, is what it is.

"Has anyone come and talked to you today?"

I shake my head. "If they did, I was asleep. These pain meds are killing me."

"Do you want them to stop giving them to you?"

"I'd like to taper off. I don't want..."

I'm overwhelmed by everything I don't want.

Again, I am completely overtaken by the unfairness of it all. Here I am, pumped full of drugs, which I've avoided all my life, because I'm doing my best to be better than my dad.

To be someone that I can be proud of, even if I'm not a Boy Scout or anything.

"We can talk to the doctor about that today," my mom says.

"Yeah," I say. "I'd like that. I just... I want to get out of here. I need to get out of here."

"Hopefully, you can. Soon. But not at the expense of your safety."

"I just don't like being cooped up like this."

"The house back in Gold Valley is ready for you. I do think you're probably going to need some extra help, though."

"I'm not going to need extra help."

"Odds are you're going to be on crutches for at least three months."

Crutches. For three months. That makes my stomach burn. I've never walked on crutches before, but I've seen other people do it. It looks labored and slow, and I can already feel my own impatience pushing against that. I can already feel my own irritation at the whole thing.

"You've never liked being patient," my mom says.

I snort. "Who *likes* to be patient? Maybe some people are better at it than others, but does anybody like waiting for what they want?"

"I think some people have a little bit more acceptance for what life is bringing to them. But you never have." She looks sad. "It can be a good thing. I know. It's been a good thing for you, sometimes, Colt. Because you've made a lot of yourself. Because that irritation and agitation that you feel has pushed you to be exceptional. I know it has."

"Yeah. So exceptional."

"Maybe it won't be a bad thing. You having to sit for a little bit and just... Take what you get. Even for a moment.

You're always doing something. Always moving on to the next thing. Maybe it won't be bad for you to sit and try to figure out exactly what else you might be able to get out of life."

"I don't want much of anything else out of life. I want to win."

"There's more to life than winning."

It's a very good, very mom thing to say, but my mom wouldn't know anything about that. She's great. She's strong and ambitious, and she's my inspiration in many ways, but she's not competitive. She has a gentle spirit, and mine is a restless one. I fear very much that I got it from my dad, and part of me hates that she has to see that on me or anyone else.

Because he just sucks so damn much.

He's famous, sadly. Like, in a niche way. Robert Campbell – bull rider.

He was a big deal in the early 2000s. Endorsement deals with every western wear company out there. Chewing tobacco, cigarettes, beer, you name it, he had his mug plastered all over the ad.

A mug that looks an awful lot like mine.

He was part model, part bull rider, all fuckboy.

He moved through towns and women leaving wreckage in his wake.

And in my case, a bastard kid he never wanted to deal with.

It's a weird thing, to look so much like a man you've barely ever spoken to. To carry a legacy in your face, your veins, especially into a venue where people do know him.

I feel obligated to keep my mouth shut about my lack of relationship with him. I don't play up that he's my dad – but we share a last name, and we share genes that can't be denied.

We also share more than that. Our ambition, our sport.

I try to take that restless spirit and add *do no harm* to it, at least.

At least I don't have a kid to let down and abandon. I fuck around, but I use a condom so that I don't have to find out. If I'm going to be a rolling stone, I need to make sure that I'm not running other people over.

I feel really strongly about that. I know what I am, but I also know not to hurt other people with it.

My dad also never won the championship. Not once.

He wasn't as famous for winning as he was for being pretty, and I want to be famous for both. But I can't do that if I don't get out of here.

There's a knock at the door, and we look up to see a doctor standing there. And so begins my physical therapy, which makes me want to punch everybody in the facility right in the face. It's painful, and it sucks.

And that's just getting me to walk on crutches.

But it's the deal if I want to get out of the hospital, and I really need to get out of the hospital. The wound in my midsection is slowly getting better, but it is causing a huge part of the problem. If I twist wrong—and trying to maneuver on crutches, on that leg, means I twist wrong a lot —I am assaulted by shooting pains. My mom is there for all of it. My stepdad is there a lot too, along with Gentry and Allison.

It surprises me that Allison is dedicated to this. But I suppose it has to do with her being a nursing student. It makes sense when I think of it that way. She obviously finds it interesting. And she probably enjoys watching me be tortured a little bit. I can't say that I blame her. I haven't always been nice to her.

There is a sort of false hope blooming with my potential discharge day. Because part of me keeps hoping it's a finish line of sorts. That it's a sign things might get back to normal, and yet I can still feel how busted my body is.

I might be headed out of the hospital soon, but I'm not headed back to anything that looks like my life.

The little house in town is fine, and I don't hate it, but it isn't me. I'm not destined to live in a suburban cage. I want to have my own land. My own ranch. But right now, even if I had that, I wouldn't be able to work it. Even if I had that, I wouldn't have the capacity to do anything with it.

My frustration is like a boiling, burning thing in my already slashed-apart midsection.

But I know there's nothing I can do about it, even as the anger builds inside of me.

I find out pretty quickly that there are no points for a good attitude. Anger doesn't help, but it certainly doesn't stop me from making progress. And if anything, it gives me an invisible enemy to fight, and that's not the worst thing.

When I finally make it to discharge day, six full weeks after the accident, I feel a certain sense of triumph. But it's limited.

Because the life that I have waiting for me out there is nothing like the life that I want. Nothing like the life I had before.

I might not be trapped in a hospital anymore, but I'm going to be trapped in Gold Valley.

I'm going to be trapped in a life I didn't choose.

And other than flat out dying, that's pretty much the worst thing I can imagine.

Chapter Six

Allison

"They're discharging him today."

My stomach jumps. Colt has worked so hard to get to this point. It's been six weeks since his accident, since the surgery, and he's come a long way from the man who was completely trapped in bed until only recently. The one who was clinging to his life when he was first brought to the hospital in Tolowa.

He got his rigid cast cut off, he's in a flexible brace that allows him to bend his knee and lets his skin breathe a little – but he can't take it off or get it wet.

He can walk with crutches now — sort of — after using a wheelchair for about a month.

I'm trying to imagine him alone in his house just a couple of doors down from mine, and it gives me a weird amount of anxiety. I can't really say why.

"I need you to do me a favor," my stepmom says, reaching out and grabbing my hand as we stand there in the hospital hallway. "Help take care of him. If I hover, he's going to start to resent me."

Shock is rolling through me. "But he already resents me."

"He doesn't," she says. "I know you two haven't had the most cordial relationship over the years, but you're a nursing student. I think it will feel less like a family member thinking he can't do things, and more like something valid."

"Right."

I can't deny that she's right, and I didn't really like the idea of him being stuck there by himself anyway. It's a good idea. It's probably a *great* idea. Because the man is stubborn and difficult, I know that. He's got a lot going on beneath the surface, despite his laid-back exterior. If you were to ask anybody about Colt Campbell, they would say that he's this wonderful, gregarious, likable guy, and that is certainly part of him.

But he's tenacious and stubborn, because you don't get to where he is in the rodeo without being that, and he hides it beneath that affable exterior.

All I can think is I'm going to be lucky if I don't get my arm bitten off while trying to take care of him.

"If you don't want to, I can have him come stay with us, or I can go stay with him in town, but I just think..."

I know he won't like that. Her instincts about her son are right, of course. He's going to have an attitude about anything that he doesn't think gives him enough credit or independence. He's going to take it as a challenge that he can't do things, and I think that has the potential to make him attempt to do things he shouldn't do. Because he's Colt, and he's too much of a risk-taker.

He always has been. He and Gentry and Dallas always

wound each other up. It's how they ended up where they are – two bull riders and a firefighter.

To be honest, I think Gentry has more sense than the rodeo cowboys. At least we need firefighters. Literally no one needs you to risk your life riding a bull.

"Of course I'll help," I say.

Because I love Cindy with my whole heart. Because she's the mother figure that I would never have had. It's always been so complicated. Her marrying my dad was such a wonderful thing. I was an adolescent, and I needed a woman in my life so badly. But she also brought Colt with her, and that was a real hallmark of difficulty for me.

I made a conscious effort to separate her being my stepmom from having to have the object of my teenage affection living down the hall from me.

But Cindy made my dad smile again. She left space for my mom while being there for me. She never tried to erase the love I had before; she only added to it.

This has been so hard on her. And I need to pull myself out of it. That's the problem. I've been a little bit too self-obsessed with all this because of how complex my own feelings for Colt are.

They don't need to be complicated. Weird... Family. I guess.

Even if that has always felt like such an uncomfortable label for the two of us.

But I can be family right now. I need to be.

I can't worry about how annoyed he's going to be with me, or how difficult it's going to be for us to have that kind of proximity. It's not like we haven't had it before. And anyway, we won't be living together, so there's that.

"Of course, if he gives you any trouble, let me know. And I'll scold him."

I laugh. "I'm sure he won't."

I drove his truck here to the hospital when he was moved from Medford, and it's been sitting here the whole time, which is how I end up being tasked with driving him back home that day.

I came with Cindy, and he and I live right next to each other, so it makes sense. I can tell that he's irritated when discharge includes a wheelchair, even though that's standard procedure. I can also tell that it's a window into exactly what I'm going to be dealing with when I'm doing the caregiving.

I go and get the car from the far reaches of the parking lot, and drive it up to the front doors, where I wait for the hospital staff to help him out of the chair and into the car. I can see beads of sweat on his forehead, his teeth gritted against the pain.

I can tell that the pain makes him angry.

He gets into the passenger seat and slams the door shut.

"Do you need to take a pain pill?"

"Advil. Maybe. I'm not taking anything else."

"Why not?"

"Because I don't like being out of control. And I know that I need to limit the amount of time that I'm on opiates."

"Sure," I say. "That's a real concern, and I get it. But you also have very real pain that you need to deal with."

"I don't have anything else to do but deal with the pain, Allison, so I might as well give it a nice warm hug and tell it to make itself comfortable."

I don't roll my eyes visibly, and I consider that to be a real triumph.

"You don't need to martyr yourself on top of everything else," I say, waving at Cindy as we pull away from the curb.

"I'm not," he says.

He's smiling, but I can hear the anger in his voice.

"I would've thought you'd be happy that you're headed home."

"Different view, same prison. These injuries. I just want to get back out on the circuit."

"But you know that's not happening," I say softly as we pull out of the hospital parking lot and onto the road. It's about a forty-minute drive back to Gold Valley, and I'm going to be stuck with this surliest of passengers.

"Yes, I'm aware of that," he says. "I'm not stupid. But I'm not happy about it either."

"You definitely don't have to be happy about it."

"Thanks," he says. I'm not sure for a second if he's thanking me for giving him permission to be mad or what. Then he continues. "For being there for all of this. You didn't have to do that."

I debate whether or not to tell him that I've been tasked with his further care and keeping, and decide now isn't the time. "Of course," I say.

"No. I get that I'm not... The most fun to be around right now. And hell, you've never been particularly excited to be around me."

"That's not true," I say.

It's not. There was a time when being around Colt Campbell made my entire week. When Gentry would bring him over for dinner, and I would just sit there eating meatloaf, staring at him. Until he became my stepbrother, and it ruined that.

"I expect you weren't dying to have another older brother."

"You probably didn't want a younger sister."

"No," he says. "I always wanted a family. I mean, and everything was great with my mom, don't get me wrong.

But... Something was missing. Also, my mom has been a hell of a lot happier since she married your dad."

"Same with my dad."

We're saying all these nice things, talking about the situation, but it doesn't really touch us. The way that our relationship has always been kind of difficult.

But he and I don't really do civil conversation, and we definitely don't do deep dives into what makes each other tick.

I decide that it's better now to just go ahead and tell him.

"Your mom asked me to check in on you. Because it's really either me, or you move home with your parents, or the hospital sends people by."

I look over at him, at his profile. The stitches on his forehead are gone, but there's an angry red line remaining, and I wonder how bad the scar will be.

He's still so handsome, and if anything, I think the scar is going to make him a little bit less pretty, add to the masculine, rugged energy that he has.

It's really unfair. He's perfect, even ruined. That's quite something.

"Yeah, seems reasonable."

I don't think he thinks so at all. I can tell that he's angry. But I have a feeling that it's not at me. Or even at his mom. Just at everything.

He's always had an intensity, just beneath the surface, and sometimes I feel like other people don't see it. Hell, I know they don't. Because everybody always talks about how nice he is. In fact, one of my friends called him a golden retriever once. And I can't think of anything less true than that. Golden retrievers are happy to stay in their yard and play fetch. To chew on a ball unbothered, and to get scratched behind the ears.

Colt isn't content. That's one of the last words I would ever use to describe him. I don't think anybody who's so obsessed with a career like his could ever be called content. The competitiveness, the danger, all of it, suggests someone striving for the next thing. And none of that happens by accident.

Nothing he's ever done has been by accident.

It feels like his intensity is closer to the surface right now, though. Like almost anyone could see it, and that isn't normal. That's something I haven't seen before. A way of being that just isn't typical Colt. Of course, how could he be his normal self? I've been so focused on whether or not he was going to survive that I guess I didn't really sit with the reality of him having to heal.

He's just not the kind of guy who's going to ever want to sit and let grass grow beneath his feet, and he has to for a little while.

And I'm going to be his babysitter.

"So, you're about halfway through school?"

I almost have whiplash from the switch in conversation. Now he wants to make small talk?

"Yes," I say.

"That's great."

"Thanks."

I tighten my hands on the steering wheel and stare straight ahead. I'm so rarely alone with Colt. It's not really by design. I haven't thought this much about my relationship with him in a really long time. About all the stages that we've gone through. About all the feelings. It's just the near-death experience that brought it all up.

"This is weird," he says.

"What is?"

"I'm used to..." He looks out the window, and we pass a sign that says Welcome to Gold Valley. And I can fill in the blanks. He's used to a hero's welcome. A triumphant return. He's used to being Colt Campbell, the Golden Boy of Gold Valley.

It isn't that he's *not*, but I can understand why he feels like things are different now. I can't imagine Colt sitting still. He's active. He always has been. I have a hard time imagining him resting. He's not the kind of guy who would ever do an office job. Not of his own accord. So, he isn't going to be working during this time.

He likes to be outside. He works with the animals, with the land. But depending on how he heals, he's going to have to rethink. I suspect he hasn't gone that far yet. I doubt he let himself.

I don't want to think about it. I don't want to have that ugly truth sitting inside of me. That his life probably changed forever that day, and there's nothing he can do about it. There's no overachieving, no being blessed or golden or lucky that's going to change it.

It'll just be what it is. And only time will tell.

Both of us fall silent as we drive into town. Our houses are just a block away from Main Street. From all the little boutique shops that tourists love in Gold Valley.

It's such a great town to walk in and walking down the street is going to be difficult for him now.

My stomach clenches. I know what it's like to have your life change when you don't want it to.

But my mom had cancer for a long time. I could see the change coming toward me for a long time. I didn't want to believe it, of course. Nobody wants to believe that a diagnosis like that is final – regardless of what you're told. We hoped, until the end. And then we did our very best to make that last bit of time as wonderful as possible.

But God, we all wanted more.

I know what it's like to have everything changed. But change came for Colt like a freight train, and I'm sure that can't be easy.

One thing I really know, though, is how you can't negotiate with things like that. They come for you. Vicious and horrible, a rabid dog going straight for your throat, whether you're ready or not.

But Colt isn't one of those people who accepts. Not easily. It's one of the things that drew me to him back when we were younger and *not* related by marriage. Now, I can see where it might benefit him, but it's also going to be difficult.

We drive down the side street that leads to our houses. Mine is white, with flower boxes underneath the windows filled with red geraniums, matching red shutters providing a punctuation mark to the crisp paint.

Colt's is also pretty, though I know it's not because he likes it that way. It's because he keeps it up for his mom and does improvements whenever she asks him to in exchange for living there when he's in town.

It's white with black trim, and a lovely potted palm on the front porch, and looks like a far more mature person lives in it.

I don't say that, though, as I steer his truck into the empty driveway.

"Do you think you can manage to get out of this beast on your crutches? Because if you flatten me, I'm not going to be able to help either of us."

He looks at me, a scowl twisting his handsome face.

"I'm fine."

I scrunch my nose. "Are you, though?"

I'm choosing violence, apparently. It's all I seem to know how to do with him. Even when I don't really mean to. It's a learned reaction at this point. A choreographed dance. Pirouette, insult, plié, snarky comment, spin, keep him five steps away at all times, pas de bourrée and jazz hands!

"I swear to God, Allison."

He begins to open the passenger door, and I quickly turn off the truck engine.

"What are you doing?" I unbuckle as quickly as possible, prepared to dive out of the truck. "Chill the fuck out, dude. Let me help you."

"You just said you didn't want me to flatten you."

"I *don't*. Which is why we're going to do it slowly, and carefully."

"Title of your sex tape?"

Those words send a broad sweep of heat over my body, and he looks at me, our eyes meeting. I feel my face getting hot, getting red, I resent that. I resent that his stupid universal punchline joke has the power to make me turn red like it's a personal thing. Like it's something I should give even one thought to. It affects me, though, and I can't deny it. And then I see something in his blue eyes. A glint of something that surprises me. But just as I begin to identify it, it's gone.

I take a sharp breath.

"It's the title of *your* sex tape," I mutter as I get out of the driver's seat.

As comebacks go, it's not a great one. But whatever, I'm working with what I've got.

I straighten my shoulders and head around to his side of the vehicle. I open up the door, and he looks down at me.

"Very chivalrous," he says.

"I'm helping you in a medical capacity," I say as I stare at him.

The corner of his mouth tips up just slightly, and even though I can tell he's uncomfortable, angry, and using poking at me to disguise it, he appreciates me saying that. I have a feeling the medical capacity part makes it feel a little bit more bearable. Versus feeling like I'm a big, strong prospector lifting him out of the carriage. Which is kind of funny.

He hands me his crutch, and then a second one.

"You know," I say. "If your truck wasn't a giant monument to masculine insecurity, this wouldn't be quite so difficult."

He's too close to me all of a sudden. Leaning over, his face only a few inches from mine. "Insecurity? Is that what you got from this?"

"Conventional wisdom says that the bigger a man's truck is, the smaller his –"

He doesn't cut me off, and it annoys me, because I don't want to say the word penis, and I think he knows that. I break off, as if I got the interruption that I was hoping for.

"My dick is fine," he says.

"Great. Thanks for that."

"I'm not breaking any records. But you know, I don't give it much thought."

"*Thank you.*"

And somehow, I know that the way he doesn't protest too much or even a little, even at all, is an indicator that, in fact, he's well above average. Because any man with an insecurity would overcompensate in this moment, and he just looks wryly amused.

I don't want to think about that. I've never found the

size of a man's penis to matter, anyway. In fact, I've never given it much thought. The first time I did, because it was uncomfortable, and it did hurt. But I couldn't say that the men I've slept with were appreciably different in size from one another.

Not that there's been a pack of them, but I'm not a prude.

I've had relationships with a few different guys, and mainly, sex feels like the thing that happens after we have dinner, that makes us a couple and not friends. Sometimes it's more fun than others, but then, sometimes I can actually get there fast enough to have an orgasm when they do. Otherwise, it's fine to just be close.

I haven't had sex in a couple of months, but it's fine, and I don't need to be thinking about it right now. I think about Brady for a moment, though, and his penis. Because it would be nice to picture a penis that isn't Colt's, which I've never seen, and I don't want to see it.

Oh God.

I need to stop thinking about this.

I can't even picture Brady's penis, and I last saw it three months ago. So really, size doesn't matter, and penises are kind of a non-event, and yet, I have been standing here staring at my stepbrother thinking about them for forty-five whole seconds.

It has to stop.

"Just let me help you down." I plant his crutch firmly in front of him, then the other one. "If you can sort of brace yourself on that, and my shoulder, and use both to get down."

"Okay. I'm taking this as medical advice, which means I'm going to sue you for malpractice if I get hurt."

"I mean, good luck with that, Colt. It would take you

about two minutes to drain my bank account and spend everything I have."

He leans in and, without sufficient warning, begins to lower himself down. I brace myself and stand firm as he manages to bring himself down to the ground with what seems like relative ease to me.

"And suddenly, I'm grateful that I've spent the past ten years lifting weights," he says. "Though, I don't love having that validated. I'd like to let myself go to seed at some point."

"Yeah. I'm sure the upper body strength helps," I say.

And then I look up, and we're not even multiple inches apart. We are a breath away from one another. He's looking at me. Gazing into my soul, I swear to God. My heart is beating so hard I feel like I might choke on it. I look up, above his eyes, at that mean scar, and without thinking, I begin to lift my hand and let it hover there, right over it.

Then I catch myself and jerk it back down to my side on an indrawn breath.

I can't just touch him. I know better than that.

"It looks better," I say. "The cut on your head. Than it *did*, I mean."

"It's my understanding that's how healing works." His voice sounds rough.

"Yeah," I say. "It just takes time."

"I'm fine," he says.

"Okay."

I move away from him, and with his keys in my pocket, lead the way to the door, where I unlock it and open it up for him. I gaze around the small, crowded living room, which was entirely furnished by Cindy, or it wouldn't be this well coordinated.

I'm rarely at Colt's house when he's there.

I've been before to check the mail, bring it in, and put it on the table when he's traveling, and I've been to check on things when Cindy has concerns about the rental. But that's it. Now I'm looking at it, and critically. The walkways are distressingly narrow for somebody trying to navigate on crutches, and I worry that he might fall.

"We need to get you a life alert," I say.

He turns and shoots me a deadly glare.

"Hey. When you've fallen and you can't get up, don't complain at me because you chose to ignore my very sterling medical advice."

"Get wrecked, Allison."

"You already did."

I walk into the kitchen, ignoring him now, and I open up the fridge. He's got nothing in there except a bottle of beer and an onion.

"This is pathetic."

"I haven't been home for months," he says.

"I know. Still, I... I'll do a grocery delivery order for you, but until then, can I just bring you dinner tonight?"

"Sure," he says.

"I'll probably make something like spaghetti. I'm not a gourmand."

"I appreciate it," he says.

The sincerity weirds me out. Normally, he would fire back a quip of some kind about my cooking, or how he already had one near-death experience this month and doesn't need to add another with my culinary skills. The simple thank you is extremely weird. I hear him walking away, and I decide to follow to see exactly where he's headed.

He takes the short trek to the living room, then turns away from the couch, standing in front of it, bracing on his crutches, his leg in a brace that makes it so stiff and straight that maneuvering is a challenge. I can see him doing the mental gymnastics on how exactly he's supposed to sit down without falling down.

"I can help you," I say.

He snorts, then lowers himself slowly, until the very end, where he loses some of his control and drops. "Fuck!"

"Well, I would've helped you," I say.

"If I hadn't torn open my fucking midsection on top of everything else, I would've been able to do it. It's harder to control your body when you don't have core muscles left intact."

"Sorry."

"Did *you* tear me open with your horns?"

"I don't think so," I say.

"Then I don't need you to apologize to me. So stop. And don't look at me like you feel bad for me. You don't even like me."

"I don't...dislike you."

"You'd rather cut your finger and rub a lemon on it than hang out with me, and we both know it. So don't go making sad puppy eyes at me now."

I know it's pain and frustration making him grumpy, but it galls me a little bit. I have been helping him. I'm not his enemy.

I'm also aware that he's reacting from a place of raw emotion right now, so I can be sanguine about it if I choose to be. And I should choose to be.

It's nearly three o'clock, and I should go home and cook. But the idea of leaving him even for a little bit gives me anxiety. I just don't know if he's going to fall somewhere weird and not be able to get up, or... Honestly, he quit taking his pain pills, and the pain of what he's going through is severe enough that I wouldn't be surprised if he moved the wrong way and lost consciousness. Yes, he's healed up quite a bit since the incident first happened, but that's not the same as being healed. Genuinely not.

"I'm just going to go get some things and cook over here."

"Why?"

I grit my teeth. "So, you don't die. Like you, dislike you or extreme indifference you, Colt, I don't want you to die."

"They discharged me from the hospital, so I don't think I'm on death's door."

"I know, but it was also on the understanding that someone would be taking care of you, and I don't feel good dumping you off and running. Usually I do a portion of spaghetti and then I freeze the rest, but I'll just make a whole batch tonight and leave you with the leftovers."

"A lot of times I just get takeout," he says.

"You can have takeout if you want," I say, looking at him closely.

"You can cook."

I wonder if he's scared at all. If anywhere inside of himself, he's had the realization that it is possible for him to hurt himself worse. That he might not be able to just navigate things the way that he wants to. Or if he's just being Colt about it. Hardheaded, stubborn, and completely sure that, for him, everything will work out just fine.

"I'll be right back."

When I go outside, close the door behind me, and start the short walk over to my place, I burst into tears. I don't even try to question it.

Chapter Seven

Colt

The house is quiet, and I hate that I feel almost desperate for Allison to come back. I'm fine.

I'm fucking fine.

The hospital discharged me, after all. And maybe I don't have the fine art of sitting while using crutches, but I'll figure it out. I'm not fragile. A fall's not going to break any more bones. Yeah, it might hurt. It's guaranteed to hurt, but pain is just pain. It's only a feeling.

I sit there, staring at the wall, remembering that moment when I fell off the bull. It's been hazy, pretty fuzzy, not ultimately an entirely clear memory, but it is right now. I can feel the horn getting under the edge of my helmet, making contact with my forehead.

The slicing, searing pain.

Yeah. I feel that.

And then I feel this cold, wrenching fear. I wasn't aware

of it fully at the time, but I feel it now. It's bad enough that I could die.

I really feel the way he tore my midsection open right then. All the blood. God, there was so much blood.

Why is this all hitting me right now? I hate it.

I just want to be fine. I just want to be fine. I didn't choose any of this.

You kind of did when you signed up to be a bull rider.

No. Pretty much everybody's fine. It's not like there's a massive mortality rate being a bull rider. More fishermen die every year.

The ocean is a fuckton more dangerous. Still, I almost died in an arena. I almost died.

I almost died.

And what is this? What the fuck is this? Sitting on my couch and all this pain, feeling freaked out and sorry for myself? Worrying about whether or not I'm going to be able to pee on my own.

What is that, if not dying a little bit?

At least, some version of myself is dead. The one that did all this without thinking twice. My stepbrother goes off and fights wildfires, and that seems reasonable, to me because I'm a bull rider, after all.

And Allison is going to become a nurse.

We risk our lives, she's going to get a job where she's going to save them.

There is no metaphor in that. I'm a dumbass.

The minutes stretch by slowly. I just want her to come back so that I don't have to sit here with my echoing thoughts. I'm rarely alone. On the rodeo circuit, I'm always surrounded by friends, fellow riders. At night, I usually have a woman in my bed. Women like a man who takes risks, and I am happy to have their admiration as a side effect of the job. When I'm home, I don't go to bed alone if I don't want to. There's a roster of women I've known since high school who like to get it on now and then. It's fun. I look down at my leg. If I were going to be with someone now, they'd have to do most of the work.

Well. My mouth still works just fine.

Pretty sure my cock is okay. That's when I realize I haven't had an erection in weeks, which is fucking odd. But nothing has felt all that sexy.

I go back to the moment when I got out of the truck. I felt a stirring of something then. When I was teasing Allison about sex tapes, and was close enough to smell the way her skin is scented like flowers.

But that is messed up, and I don't even have pain meds as an excuse for that because I quit them cold turkey.

My front door opens, and Allison comes back in carrying a couple of canvas bags.

"I brought some Kombucha."

"Oh, *fuck me,*" I say.

"I'm kidding. I brought Coke. But you have beer anyway."

"I like a Coke with dinner," I say, knowing that I sound a little bit whiny.

"I know you do," she says. "I lived with you for almost three years, remember?"

Yeah. I do remember. And I know she's not actually asking.

It's a relief that she's not being saccharine. I don't think I can handle that. Because I feel fragile, which is ridiculous. I'm a lot of things, but fucking fragile isn't one of them.

But all those memories are hovering so close to the surface, and I am just really grateful that she's here. That

I'm not by myself with my echoing thoughts. Because what a nightmare.

"Do you want to come into the kitchen while I cook?"

"No thanks. But I will watch some TV. If you'll get the remote for me. Since you're here to care for me and all."

I'm doing it to be annoying, but that's when I realized that I really don't want to hunt for the television remote, because it would require me moving, and now that I'm down on the couch, I don't especially want to get up. I don't like that feeling at all. The feeling that moving would be so much more effort than staying still. It's just not me.

It's really not.

She doesn't respond to it either way; she just grabs it off the console and throws it in my direction.

"I'll come get you when dinner is ready."

Baseball is on, and I can work with that. It's not my favorite sport, but hell, I'll watch golf if it's the only thing that's on. Football is my drug of choice, but it's not that time of year yet.

So I'll watch the Dodgers walk all over another team for a few hours.

I can hear her moving around in the kitchen, and I find it oddly soothing.

For all that I hook up a lot, I'm not one for cohabitation-type stuff. It just makes me feel... I don't know.

The idea of permanence makes my skin crawl.

I know marriage was great for my mom, honestly. But everything that she went through before that... It was just terrible. I had to be the man of the house at a really young age, and all the stuff with my dad... It just put me off. And I stay off of it.

I'm never going to be the kind of man who can't take

care of a wife and kid. So I just won't have one. That's easy enough.

My mom and dad were never married, of course. She got pregnant, and at that point, she already had to track him down. She was open with me about that. And she got really candid about prophylactics.

She was only nineteen when she had me. And I feel like it was brave of her, the way she weathered it. Honestly, whatever she did would've been brave. She chose to keep me, and I'm grateful to her for that. I'm not grateful to my dad for a damn thing.

And I'll never, ever be him.

I turn my thoughts back to the game, but it's a blowout, and it's not holding my attention. Still, before I realize it, Allison has appeared in the doorway with two plates of spaghetti. "I'm just going to bring it out here," she says.

"No, I can go in there."

"*No,*" she says. "I'm super into... baseball."

"You have never watched a game of baseball in your life."

"Sure, I have."

"No," I say.

"Go team," she says.

"Which team?"

"I just hope everyone has fun."

She goes and grabs a TV tray from behind the chair in the corner, sets it up in front of me like she's my good and proper nurse. But I'm starving, and in no position to get irritated at her when she's cooked for me. I mean, I could, but it would be petty. I'm a lot of things, but I'm not petty. And I'm going to do my best not to project all of my angst onto her. It's not fair. She doesn't deserve it.

She puts a Coke on the tray next to my plate of

spaghetti. I'm more grateful than I want to show, even if I don't want to be a jerk.

But I open the Coke fast enough that I'm sure she can see I'm excited about it.

She doesn't sit on the couch near me; instead, she sets up her tray in front of the chair.

"Your mom said she's been texting you?"

Shit. I haven't even looked at my phone.

"Oh." I reach into my pocket, and I take my phone out. Dammit. She's sent me a string of texts and is getting increasingly worried. I respond that Allison is with me, and she made me spaghetti, and it's fine. Even though I have a feeling Allison already told her that.

This way, maybe she won't think I only checked my phone because of Allison.

"I'm surprised she didn't move in."

"If I hadn't agreed to look after you, she would have."

I grimace. That tracks. "Thanks. I love my mom. Don't get me wrong. But I don't exactly want to cohabitate with her."

"Fair enough. I love my dad, but I don't want to move back in with him."

"Yeah. Well, I think my mom would mean well and do everything in her power to stop me from getting a hangnail at this point. So, I wouldn't be allowed to do anything for myself." I try to say that with no irony, but given I'm sitting here being served by her, and she even got the TV remote for me, I feel a little bit stupid.

"She loves you."

I laugh. "Oh. I know. I'm not under any illusion that my mom doesn't love me. I'm lucky that way."

She nods. "Yeah. You really are. Your mom is the best. I'm lucky too."

Parents are such a thorny topic. Her real mom is dead. My real dad is just a horrible human being, and the fact of the matter is, we're both lucky our parents met and married. Honest truth.

But, it's still thorny. I don't often sit in the thorns. I'm usually too busy moving on to the next thing.

Ohtani hits a home run, and she points to the TV. "That was good. I know enough to know that was good."

"You're practically ready for the MLB now."

"Yep. That's me. Very athletic."

I never thought of her as unathletic, but she was definitely more inside than out. When she was really little, back when she was just my friend's little sister, she used to trail after us on her dad's property, following Gentry and me all around, and complaining loudly whenever she was made to be even a little bit uncomfortable. She didn't like bees, she didn't like getting her feet wet, didn't like it when she got burrs in her socks.

I can't say that I like any of those things, but we were twelve-year-old boys with an annoying nine-year-old trailing after us, and I would have pretended that I love nothing more than to stick my right hand into a beehive and my left ankle into a sludgy pond if it meant demonstrating my toughness in the face of her whining.

I suppose that's a pretty good indicator of how we ended up with the relationship we have.

She was always just a kid, irritating to me, and I didn't hide it. If she'd had pigtails, I'd have pulled them.

I look up, and she's got her gaze fixed on the TV, her face in profile. She's beautiful. Her nose reminds me of a ski slope, sweet freckles sprinkled across it, all around her cheeks. She used to hate them when she was little, and now

I've seen girls paint freckles on their faces because they're so trendy. It's funny how that stuff happens.

She's got that striking red hair. Copper mixed with deep, russet tones. Her hair isn't really curly. It isn't really straight. It's a mix of the two, and often does its own thing. She keeps it in a messy bun a lot of the time, which, right now, she has it down, tumbling over her shoulders.

If I think about pulling her hair now, it has a whole different undertone.

Oh. Hell. No. No. I'm not going there.

"This is great," I say, because interrupting my thoughts seems like a good move at this point.

"You were just in a hostage situation with hospital food for weeks."

I snort. "Right. That is true. But this is still good."

"Thank you. My left wrist really got a workout opening that jar."

My brain stalls out, trying to make a joke about the last time my left wrist got a workout, though given that I was just reflecting on the fact I haven't had a hard-on in weeks, there's not much to say. And anyway, I shouldn't say it in front of her. There was something...

There was something when I made that joke about the sex tape. Then she started talking about pickup trucks and penises.

Well, she didn't actually say the word.

She turned bright red, though. And the trouble is, it's not like harassing her when she was young. I used to get a kick out of her face turning red because I knew she was annoyed at me. Now it makes me think of other things. Because she's not a kid, she doesn't look like a kid. She's a woman. And when her cheeks turned pink, I think of...

God damn. I wonder if I can actually call one of the

women that I normally hook up with and see if she wants to help me with one of those erections. Because if my brain is going there, that means I'm hard up. Even if my physical body hasn't fully realized it.

This is Allison. My stepsister.

Beehives. Pond sludge. Stepsister.

Getting gutted by a bull.

There. One of those ought to do it.

Of course, if I call one of those women, they're going to look at me with pity in their eyes rather than lust.

Damn. That does it. Turned off. No. I don't want to be pitied. That is not who I am. I'm Colt Campbell, and I've always gone after what I wanted. I've always been an object of admiration. Pity? No. Never.

"Do you have any grocery delivery apps on your phone?"

It's such a banal question in contrast with what I was thinking.

"No?"

"How do you survive?"

"Half the year on the road, and half the year subsisting like a basement possum scrounging around for whatever I can find, going out to the bar, going out to the other bar, going out to Mustard Seed..."

"Well, I'm going to make a grocery order for you. I'll bring everything over tomorrow and I'll put it away."

"That sounds perilously close to you being my housekeeper."

"I'm not. I have a job. And I'm going to school. So, I'm a little bit too busy to be your housekeeper, but I can keep you alive."

"I can place my own grocery order; you just have to tell me what service I want."

"And you're going to put everything away?"

I don't like that. Because putting groceries away is nothing, but right now it sounds like so much work. Right now, it sounds like something I would really struggle to do, and it just seems so basic.

"How about this, I'll put a grocery order to my house, I'll have some things for you, I'll put it away, and I'll make you dinner again tomorrow night."

"I don't like it."

"Yeah, but you're not going to like much of anything right now."

That comment kills what I was going to say next. It outright dies on my tongue. Because she's right. I don't like any of this. So yeah, I'm not going to like her coming over and fixing dinner. I'm not going to like her doing food deliveries, her basically taking care of me. But also, it's probably not smart of me to waste the energy that I have on small things. Maybe.

Not that I'm sure what I have that energy for.

She stays to watch the game, but we don't do much talking. And then, the doorbell rings.

"I'll get it," she says.

"Thanks," I say. This is the millionth time I've had to thank her sincerely in a way too short an amount of time. But I'm reminded yet again that I'm not going to like anything right now.

"It's Dallas. And Sarah." She jerks the door open, and the enthusiastic sounds of greetings happen behind my head. I could turn, but I'm feeling tired. My body is starting to ache. I'm an old man.

That thought gives me enough impetus to turn my head. "Hey," I say.

"Oh, Colt." Sarah is looking at me like I'm a sad baby chicken.

That is the exact look I didn't want to see on the face of a woman I wanted to hook up with. I don't want to hook up with Sarah. I didn't want to hook up with Sarah because when I met her, I thought she was pretty and interesting, and I'm the kind of person who gets along well with women even after we've slept together.

But obviously that wasn't to be. Since she and Dallas were soulmates from way back. I didn't know that when I was hitting on her.

And we never did sleep together, so her pity shouldn't hurt. But it does.

"I'm fine," I say, which is not true. I'm not fine.

"I'm glad you're home," says Dallas, stuffing his hands in his pockets."

"Yeah. Me too."

"This is why I'm glad you quit," Sarah says, grabbing Dallas by the arm.

"That's insensitive," I say. "To those of us who didn't quit and got injured."

She looks stricken. "Sorry."

"I'm kidding."

She still looks sorry she said it. And you know, I'm kind of here for that. Is it demonstrably different than pity? Am I being ridiculous? I feel like I have the right.

"Come in," Allison says. "Sit down."

"Yeah. Come in. Sit down. It's almost like it's your house."

"It's not. But you can't get up," she says.

"I can get up."

"So," Dallas says, ignoring my conversation with Allison. "What's the prognosis?"

"Oh. I'll be back to normal in a few months."

I can feel Allison staring at me. That's not what anyone said. But I don't want to get into what was said. I don't like it. It's uncertain, and all it's going to get me is more questions, more sad eyes. Offers of help, all kinds of things, I just don't want to deal with.

"So, back to it next year?"

I think of the way that I was ground into the arena dirt, the feeling of the horn tearing through my body. "Yeah. I'm not going to be done until I win. And fucking Maverick has a pretty clear field without you or me. I'm almost tempted to tell you to go back. Though I know that would be an unpopular decision."

Sarah looks murderous. "It would be a widow-making decision. I'm too young to be a widow."

"You're not married," I say.

"Yeah. But we will be," Dallas says, smiling at her. I like that my friend is in love. It's a good thing. It also makes me feel like I'm on the outside of something that I can't understand, which feels unfair, really. Dallas spent the first fifteen years of his life in foster care. He didn't end up in a conventional family until he was a teenager, but somehow he's in a great relationship.

Maybe because he knew her back then. Because she was always there.

I don't know. I can't claim expertise on this or anything else. Not as far as relationships go, anyway.

They stay for a while and shoot the breeze, and I'm reluctant to show how exhausted I'm getting, but sitting up, talking, engaging, while totally off of pain meds is fatiguing in a way I didn't fully account for.

And it's Allison who notices.

"You should probably get some rest," she says.

"I'm fine," I say. Knowing full well that it's a lie.

"Oh yeah," Dallas says. "It's good to see you... Out of the hospital."

"It's good to be out of the hospital."

Dallas claps my shoulder, and Sarah does the same, before the two of them leave.

I decide to turn some of my irritation onto Allison, and I know it's not fair. Even as the words exit my mouth, I know it's not fair. I decide to do it anyway.

"I don't need you to babysit me."

"You don't? Because you're over-exhausting yourself and you just lied to your best friend."

"No, I didn't," I say. Which is dumb, because she was there, and she knows full well that I lied.

"You really believe that you're going to be back at it in a few months?"

I stare at the back wall. "That's not anything that I need to think about right now."

"I think it would be good if you did. I think it's probably smart for you to try and figure out what things might look like in six months."

"No, thank you. You know what, I am tired, and I think you should go home."

She lowers her brows, her forehead creasing. "Don't do this. Don't be mean to me just because I know what's going on with you."

"You know what's going on with me? That's kind of a trick. Considering I don't know what's going on with me."

"Whatever. Good night." She moves over to my TV tray, scoots out of my way, and takes my plate.

"I don't need you to do that."

Her eyes meet mine, a stubborn expression on her face, and she slams the plate back down on the tray. "Okay.

Enjoy cleanup. I'll be in touch with you tomorrow about groceries."

I regret everything that's come out of my mouth since Dallas and Sarah walked out the door, but I don't quite know what to do with it.

I don't know how to course correct, because it would mean backing down, apologizing. It would mean accessing the kind of sincerity that feels like it might scrape me raw now.

So I don't say anything. I just watch her collect her things and storm out of the house. And then I'm left alone. With my thoughts. With my memories. With everything that terrifies me.

And I wish I had done things differently.

Chapter Eight

Allison

As annoyed as I am, I decide to go check on him in person the next morning. I let everything he said last night get to me a little bit too deeply. I know Colt better than that. I know him well enough that I should've just breezed past all his inflammatory statements. I shouldn't have let him get under my skin. He's putting on a brave face for Sarah and Dallas, and calling him out on that was an affront to his pride, and I know Colt well enough to know he won't allow that. So why couldn't I let it go? I don't know. But I've got a stake in how badly things went last night, if only because I should respect that he's not in the best place.

But hearing him say that – hearing him say that he was going to be right back in the arena in just a few months worried me.

I don't want him to go back to riding. And not only that, I'm not sure it's possible, and the idea that he's in denial on that level frightens me.

I don't think he is, though. I kind of think he just wishes he could be.

I text him, and I don't get a response. I get dressed for the day and grab my bag of coffee beans, intent on making him some at his place. Then I have to work for about three hours at the store, put in a couple of hours of coursework, and take care of the grocery shopping, I guess.

I ring the doorbell, but he doesn't answer. And that's when I start getting worried. I fish around for the extra key that I know is hidden at the front of the house, and with some hesitation, I unlocked the door.

I hear running water in the house, the sound of the shower.

We were sent home with a few things to help him shower, but the idea of him doing it by himself...

He might've fallen. What if he's unconscious?

"Colt?" I shout his name, hoping that he'll answer, but he doesn't.

I curl my hands into fists, and I press forward. No, I don't really want to bust in on Colt's shower. But the reality is, he could be hurt. And privacy and nudity are not the utmost concerns at the moment.

His safety is.

He isn't allowed to get certain things wet, so he's been sponge bathing at the hospital, and that's sort of what he's supposed to do here, on the bench that they sent home with him, but he's so stubborn, who knows exactly what he's trying?

I followed the sound of the running water to the master bedroom, then I open up the door and see the bathroom door ajar. "Colt?"

I still don't hear an answer.

So, I take a deep breath, and I move forward, pushing

the door open. And then I nearly injured myself practically cartwheeling out of the room.

Because he's in there, just fine, sitting on the bench with water pounding down on his back, completely naked.

And even though I move in and out quickly, he raises his head, turns it, and meets my gaze. That one moment, his blue eyes boring into mine as he sits there naked - *completely naked* – is going to live in my head rent-free for the rest of my life. So is the vision of his sculpted muscles. His broad, incredible shoulders, his washboard flat midsection. His thick, solid-looking thighs, and...

The whole side view of his ass sitting on that bench is really something.

Thank God he's so muscular, because those treetrunk thighs disguised the sight of his...

But even still, as I careen back into the bedroom, I see more in my mind's eye than I should. His flat abs leading down to the hard-cut line of his Adonis belt, and a tuft of hair just above... The problem is I know exactly what's there.

As much as I don't want to think about it, I don't want to know about it... I do.

And I'm never going to be able to get the vision of him out of my head.

"Normally, I expect a tip if I put on a show like that," he calls out toward the bedroom as the water shuts off.

I grimaced. "I was worried about you," I shout.

"No need to be worried."

"I called your name."

"All I could hear was water."

I hear heavy movements in the bathroom. And he comes out on his crutches, a towel wrapped around his waist, his brace covered by a waterproof liner. This is the first time I get a real-life view of the injury on his midsection. He's not stitched back together anymore. But the scar is ugly and deep, fresh and angry-looking.

He's still way too naked for my peace of mind. And way too hot, even scarred up like this.

I can't remember ever being immobilized by the sight of a man's naked body. Colt has managed to do it, even outside of a sexual context. That seems like a superpower. What I really wish my stepbrother didn't have.

"I'm good," he says. "I didn't expect you this morning."

"I was worried. I brought... Stuff to make your coffee."

"Thanks."

I do my best not to look at him. I do my best not to let my eyes linger on his powerful thigh, very exposed with the way he's holding his towel, and his chest and abs, marred though his abs are by that scar.

Suddenly, much to my horror, I feel tears building in my eyes. He is so beautiful. And this accident has changed that beauty forever.

I swallow hard and turn away from him. I'm being weird, and he doesn't need to be exposed to that. He doesn't need to deal with me.

I rush into the kitchen and busy myself making coffee. It takes about twenty minutes for Colt to join me. But when he does, he's dressed. For him, at the moment, that means wearing jeans that are split up the side, which allow space for his brace.

"How many pairs of jeans did they ruin?"

He shrugs. "I think my mom went and got me some new Wranglers and cut about five of them."

Of course she did. I don't say anything to him about adaptive clothing or other options because the thing about Colt is, he's going to do what he's going to do.

"That's good."

"Yeah."

He maneuvers on his crutches to the breakfast nook table. Then he hoists himself down and looks at me expectantly. "If you're going to come and invade my privacy, I expect you to be full-service."

"Yeah, it's about to be," I say, going to the cabinet and taking out a coffee mug.

Then I set to preparing him a cup.

"I'm sorry about last night," he says, not looking at me.

"Oh. I didn't realize it was notable. It just seemed like you being you."

He grimaces. "What does that mean?"

"That you don't like to deal with difficult feelings. And this whole thing is rife with difficult feelings."

"Touché. But who likes dealing with stuff like this? My mom said something about how I don't like being patient. And I maintain that nobody actually likes it."

"Right. I guess that's true."

"Being injured is that enough without you all telling me how bad I am at it."

Something softens in my chest as I set the coffee mug down in front of him. "I'm sorry. I realize that... That's kind of messed up. That's not what I'm trying to do. I'm not trying to tell you that you're bad at being injured. It's just that... I guess in a lot of ways I think that what we're trying to do is show you that we understand this is difficult for you."

"Thanks." That word is dry this time, and he takes a sip of his coffee.

"I don't have a lot of time. I have to go start my shift at Sammy's."

Sammy Daniels is a great boss. She has the cutest

jewelry store, stocked entirely with things she makes. Sarah and I are reducing our hours as school ramps up for us both. I'm starting my clinical rotations next semester and I won't be working at all. There are a couple of new girls taking over as our school schedule ramps up. But it's where I met Sarah, and she's been a great friend. I feel really lucky to have her, and I know it's because of the jewelry store.

"Great. Don't let the door hit you on the way out."

"So now you're just going to be surly?"

"I feel kind of entitled to mood swings."

"Fair enough."

I don't leave. Instead, I pour myself a cup of coffee, and I sit down at the breakfast table across from him. "How was your night last night?"

"Terrible. I slept awful."

"Maybe there's something you could take for that."

"I don't want to. This whole thing already feels like it's out of my control. I don't want to end up taking a whole bunch of stuff –"

"Colt, accidents are always out of people's control. There's no shame in taking something to help you through it."

"I don't need to. I'm just going to... It'll be fine."

"It is going to be fine. But it might be different."

There's something steely in his gaze then. "I'm going to get back to normal. As close to that as I can. Nothing else is acceptable."

"Why?"

He looks at me. "Because. Because I can't imagine being like this for the rest of my life."

"What does that mean?" I'm so sad that he feels this way. But there's something about this that makes him feel so desperately helpless and not himself. It's understandable, I guess. But there's no way to know the future. There's no way to know how he's going to be after this.

I know he doesn't necessarily believe that it's a certainty he'll be okay, but I do worry that it's the only outcome he can accept.

"There are a lot of people in this world who have struggles, Colt. Who have physical differences and limitations. And you wouldn't think that they weren't worth something just because they couldn't do absolutely everything."

"Of course not. But that's different. It's not me. I want to be able to do the things I've always done."

"You might not be able to."

"That's great, Allison. Who doesn't want tough love with their coffee from someone who currently has two working legs?"

"Okay. You're right. I don't know what this is like. I don't understand exactly what you're going through. I care about you. I care about you, and I don't like seeing you despairing. I don't think it needs to be despair."

"You don't just tell me what my feelings ought to be."

"Okay. That's fair. But I just want you to know, what you can or can't do doesn't really change who you are. And I understand that it might feel like it does. But it doesn't really. Not to me."

"Then you don't really know me."

He was quick to apologize for last night, but the obvious truth is that his mood isn't actually any better. And I should take a cue and leave him alone.

"I need to go to work."

I take the rest of my coffee and dump it in the sink, and then I head out the front door without so much as a goodbye. I can walk to work. And I do, because I need the fresh air to clear my head. I stop at the coffee shop and get myself another drink, since I discarded mine at his place. And I was not ready to be finished.

Then I head toward the jewelry store and unlock everything before taking my position behind the counter. Sarah arrives not long after.

"Good morning."

"Good morning," Sarah says cheerfully. "How's your patient?"

"He's... You know. Him."

"He seemed optimistic last night."

"He's lying," I say. "He's not optimistic. Not about that. There's no reason to be." I feel guilty as soon as those words exit my mouth. "His injuries are really severe," I say. "It's not as simple as just waiting for the bone graft to heal and getting back to normal."

"Oh," Sarah says.

"He just doesn't want..." He hasn't even said, but I have this idea that I know what he's thinking. That I know what is making him behave the way he is.

"I think he doesn't want anyone to see him differently. He's so used to being Colt. You don't really get it, because you have only been here a few months. But he's... He's the kind of guy who turns everything he touches into gold. He's the kind of guy who smiles at something and gets it. He's never met defeat, at least not as far as I'm aware. And this is about as close as he's ever gotten. I don't think he's weathering it very well."

"Well," Sarah says, resting her elbows on the jewelry case. "I can understand that. In the sense that nothing ever went my way, but deep down, I always believed that I was going to muscle my way out of it. I always believed that I was going to be able to overcome. Because I had to believe it. Because if I didn't believe it... Well, what's the alternative? It's just sort of sinking into despair, isn't it?"

"I don't know. It's different. You were born struggling, I think." I feel guilty talking about him like this. "The first time I ever came up against something I couldn't fight was my mom's cancer. You can't argue with diseases like that. They're going to do what they do. There are no bootstraps you can pull yourself up by. It just is. And I know that Colt knows that. I know that he understands it. But I also think that he's always been under the impression that for him things were different."

"I see." Sarah takes a deep breath, and then she straightens. "Are you okay?"

I wrinkle my nose. "Yeah. Of course."

"There's no, of course. In the last few weeks... You've been through a lot."

"Oh, please. I've barely been through anything. Not in comparison to Colt or to the rest of my family."

"But you..."

I know she knows. We haven't discussed it deeply, but she guessed it pretty quickly. Not that I was chill or subtle about it when she came to town and Colt seemed interested in her. Which was fine – in the sense that I'm used to Colt hooking up with women in my vicinity and I know my attraction to him will never amount to anything.

But I didn't handle someone who was becoming a friend being interested in him all that well. Though, it turned out she wasn't interested in him at all.

"It's okay. I don't judge you, you know. I really don't. Dallas is my foster brother. It's not even that different."

"It's pretty different," I say. I clear my throat. "Anyway. I don't have *feelings* for him. Not beyond normal, regular feelings. I just..."

"You're attracted to him."

"Yes. Exactly. But what woman isn't attracted to Colt? That doesn't make me special. And anyway, I'm taking care of him because he's family." The words burn.

"Okay. I trust you. I just wanted to make sure that you were being checked in with. Because I know that everyone has been focused on him – with good reason. But I just wanted to make sure that someone was checking in on you."

It's really sweet of her. But also makes me feel remarkably uncomfortable. Not her fault. It's the whole situation. That my feelings are really tangled up in strange ways where Colt is concerned.

That I don't like being perceived, mainly because I want to hide from myself.

"I really appreciate it. I mean, it's terrible," I say, looking down at my hands. "It's terrible to see him like this."

Sarah puts her hand on my shoulder. "It's terrible for me. I can only imagine how difficult it is for you.

"Yeah. I mean, it's hard. He's... He's always seemed unbreakable to me. Indestructible. He's larger-than-life. He always has been."

"I get it."

"Right. You almost hooked up with him."

Sarah laughs.

"I did not almost hook up with him. I had the thought that it might be nice if I could rally myself to do it, but having to rally yourself to sleep with somebody isn't a great reason to do it."

I think back on my previous relationships. About the void where Brady's penis should be. How little I care about it. Now, and then.

"It's fine," I say.

"You've said that to me before," says Sarah. "But it really *should* be ecstatic. Not fine."

I shrug, looking down at one of the rings in the case, the diamonds glittering up at me. Sparkle so brilliant and bright it could never be called just fine. "I think people are different, is all I'm saying."

"I think some men don't put a lot of effort into it. And I think chemistry plays a big role." She smiles just slightly. "You know, when I met Dallas, we were kids. So it wasn't all chemistry or anything back then. But I just... He was my person. From moment one. I just felt it. Like he was a missing part of me. Like he completed something inside me. I just really felt like we were something special from the beginning. I think sometimes you know."

"I'm sure you do. Sometimes. I'm also sure that sometimes a teenage crush is just a teenage crush, and it goes away with time."

"Yeah. I'm sure."

I don't like the way she says that, which makes me feel like she doesn't believe me at all. There's no way in hell that I was meant to have feelings for Colt. For so many reasons.

"I hope he does get back to normal," I say. "I really do. I hope that he heals completely, and he's back in the rodeo." I swallow, because that's kind of a lie, even if I wanted to be true. "And I want him to be able to just go back and be him. And if he was going to be with me... He wouldn't be able to have any of that. And if he decided to be with me because he couldn't have any of that... No. I'm not anyone's consolation prize."

The words hurt. To think them, to say them. And it's galling to even have to acknowledge my past crush, my present attraction to that degree. I'm not going to let it hurt me, though. I don't need to let it hurt me.

The reality is, he's attractive.

I saw him naked today, and my whole body about went up in flames, I can't deny that. But also, I'm very clear on who he is and who I am, and what's possible and what's not. There's the reality of just us, how I don't think we would've ever been compatible in that way. He's one of those popular people. The kind where things seem to go easy for him.

I'm not that person. My hair doesn't fall perfectly into place. I'm not effortless in any capacity. Effortless people don't date those who labor. That's just a fact. Effortless people, like him, seek out other people who have a beam of light that perpetually shines down upon them from heaven.

His sparkle would have to be dimmed for him to reach down and touch me.

I don't want that. Not for either of us.

"I think the bigger problem would be dating her stepbrother in a small town," Sarah says pragmatically.

"Well. Yeah. That sounds like an absolute nightmare. And again, one of the many, many reasons it's simply an impossibility. It's never going to be like that."

"Yeah. Okay." We have a couple of walk-ins asking for the installation of permanent jewelry. Sarah does one, and I do the other. It's a fun process that involves a welding pen, and I really enjoy it. I never considered myself creative until I started working at Sammy's. She showed me some jewelry-making techniques since she hired me, and it makes me want to make things of my own. I didn't leap in and get jewelry-making supplies, but I did get back into knitting. Which might not seem like the same thing, it's all about creating new things and putting them out in the world.

I used to knit with my mom while she got her infusions. I stopped for a long time because it just hurt. But now I can find the peace in it again.

I like that. I want to be a nurse so that I can save people. I want to create things. Cancer isn't an entity; it's a disease. It doesn't know how much I hate it. It doesn't know the destruction that it causes. It's not sentient.

Sometimes I wish it were. So that a hearty *fuck cancer* might mean something.

So the fact that I'm getting a job to help defeat something that steals, tears apart, destroys, might matter. I'm going to sit with people while they fight cancer. I'm going to help them find the strength to continue treatment, I'm going to be comforting and help them feel dignity, hope and peace.

I kind of wish cancer knew that.

But it doesn't. And it never will. So I just have to make things, including making a difference, because it matters to me.

Everything else is something you can't control.

When I get off my shift, I have a text from Cindy who wants Colt and me to come over for dinner tomorrow night if he has the energy. A family dinner, she says, with Gentry and Lily. I used to be so jealous of Lily because she got to run around with the boys. She was somehow one of them when I never was. I used to worry that Colt would fall in love with her, because she is beautiful, that is true. And I wondered if he would fall for her. Honestly, that could still happen.

I don't ruminate about that. Because it's silly. I need to stop ruminating in general.

I decide to go to the store in person, and pick up some frozen meals that will be easy for Colt to heat up for himself, some Cokes and beer, coffee for his house, and a few things to make a quick dinner. For tonight, I just get lazy and grab a precooked half rack of ribs along with some potato salad and macaroni salad. It's going to be a beige wonder of a meal, but I don't have the energy to worry about nutrition. I'll just pray over it and call it good. The thought makes me laugh, though honestly, any thought about good health at the moment for Colt makes me laugh. A lack of green vegetables is the least of his concerns.

I give him a courtesy text before I pop over again. And then I ring the doorbell about twenty times before I walk in.

When I do, he's sitting on the couch looking at me. "I'm not getting up."

"Well, I didn't want to walk in on you naked again." My bad for bringing up the nudity immediately.

"It doesn't make any difference to me. I have no modesty left. I've had nurses sponge out creases I didn't know I had."

I'm aware that that's going to be part of my job as a nurse. You have to take care of people to the best of your ability, while preserving their dignity, but sometimes dignity is just hard to come by because injury and illness can be such an undignified experience. But the people caring for you can make it better. And they can make it worse. I met so many great and terrible medical professionals during my mom's illness. And that was just me as a kid. So I can't imagine how much more intense it was for the adults, for my mom.

"Did you have good nurses?"

He frowns. "Weird question. But yes."

"It's not a weird question. This is what I want to do. I think that it's really important to have medical professionals who show you a lot of care. Even when they're sponging out creases."

"Wow. But yeah. I was really lucky, I think. Everyone was great."

"I'm glad. I'll probably end up getting work in Tolowa." I carry the bags through the room and head into the kitchen. I open up his fridge and start putting things away, then I get out plates and silverware for the dinner that I brought home.

It takes a while, but eventually he comes into the kitchen. "You're going to move away?"

"It makes the most sense. And I might not move. I might stay here. It's only a forty-five-minute drive. But maybe I'll work in the cancer center or...I don't know."

"My mom will probably see it as an excuse to get some investment properties in Tolowa."

I grin. "Yeah. Okay. Probably."

"Do you want to move?"

I shrugged. "This is the only place I've ever lived. Even moving forty-five minutes away seems weird."

"It's a good tether," he says. He sits down at the table, that leg straight out in front of him. He doesn't look quite as tired or terrible as he did yesterday. I'm relieved to see it.

"What do you mean by tether?"

"It's a place I always want to come back to. But I don't necessarily want to be here all the time."

"Right. You like traveling with the rodeo."

"I like being different all the time. We moved from Bend when I was little, but I barely remember living there. I remember we had a little house with a yard, and there was a river that ran right behind it. There was a fence, and my mom used to always warn me about climbing that fence. I didn't listen, of course."

"Well, that's terrifying. Pediatric drowning is one of the leading causes –"

"I know. But I was young and dumb and thought I was

invincible. I thought I was invincible until about three weeks ago."

Silence settles between us for a moment. There's a real heaviness to his words. He's not kidding. For a moment, I mourn the passing of that man who never considered his mortality. It was part of what made him who he was. This experience is going to change him, not just physically. It's already changed me. It introduced me to the horror of the sudden, random trauma. I was already familiar with the kind you could see coming from a mile away.

"I'll dish you some food."

"I will," he says. "I've barely been up and down all day. It'll be good for me." He stands up, slowly, and walks on his crutches over to the kitchen island, where he picks up a plate. It's hard for me not to help. I want to make it easier for him, but I know that's not what he wants. I know that what he wants is his independence back. To not have his stepsister looming around. I suppose I don't need to stay for dinner. And yet... He's the kind of man who usually goes out every night. The kind who's used to uproarious applause and traveling with a huge band of people. He's not used to being alone. I worry much more about his mental health than anything else.

I dish my own food, and then I sit down with him. The tension from this morning seems to be gone. He doesn't seem as angry.

"What did you do all day?"

"Watched TV. There are some really trash talk shows that I can't believe still exist."

"Oh. That's... Good."

"Probably not. Odds are, I'm doing serious damage to my health and wellness. Though in the case of ten-month-old Jeremy, Keith was the father."

I frown. "Was that good?"

"For Tanya. I don't think it was good for Keith."

"Hey, the comfort of truly garbage TV is sometimes the exact thing that a person needs."

"How about you?"

"We've got to do some permanent jewelry installations today. I did some studying. I have a final on Friday."

"You sure do a lot," he says.

I'm stunned by this statement. Because I would've thought that he and Gentry would see me as boring if they thought about me at all. I would've thought that they would feel like I do very little in comparison to them. Gentry fights fires, and Colt is a rodeo cowboy. I'm oddly touched that he sees what I do as being a large amount of anything.

"It's just working and going to school. A lot of people do that."

"I guess. But I'm sure that you could skip the working part-time if you wanted to."

"Yeah. Well, I'm not going to work for the last year of school. I'm finishing this term and then I start clinical rotations at the hospital so I won't be working."

"Oh, you'll actually work at the hospital while you're still in school?"

"Yeah, this program starts you a little later on rotations, but that's because I did most of my credits online. Anyway, it's been a little bit of a slower path, and I'm sure that my dad would pay for everything. But it just seems... Your mom letting me live in one of her rentals is so kind, and my dad is helping pay for my school. It's better to have a little bit of money that's mine." I look down at my plate. "I was talking to Sarah today about resilience. She was just saying that she always knew life wasn't going to treat her fairly. But she did her best to muscle it into the best-case scenario. If she can do that, then the least I can do is work and go to school. The least I can do is put my back into it for my dream."

"Yeah. Fair enough. But I'm still impressed. You couldn't have paid me to go to school any longer than I had to. And here you are, doing it by choice."

It surprises me that he's being this nice.

"Were you lonely today?"

"A little bit stir crazy, I admit. But, you know, I felt better. I feel better."

"You're not better," I say.

"I am, though. A little bit better every day. That is true. Undeniable, even."

"Well... Yes. It's true. But with everything that I know about healing, and about the kind of fracture that you got, it's a long road ahead. You are really lucky you didn't lose your leg."

He goes just a little bit pale. But he doesn't say anything. Instead, he attacks his food with even greater relish, acting like I didn't say a word.

"I'm just saying. You don't want to push yourself too hard. It's not going to make you heal faster. There's going to be a point where you're doing PT and then... That will be the time to push yourself. Until then, your job is resting."

"I hate resting," he says.

"I know."

We finish eating, and I stand up. But my foot gets tangled up in the chair, and I lose my balance, and Colt reaches out, gripping my hip and stopping me from falling flat on my face.

I'm facing him, standing in front of him, my breasts level with his eyes, his hand planted firmly on my hip.

And suddenly, my whole body goes hot.

Like I was lit on fire.

This isn't a slow smolder like the other times recently, this is something major. Something deep and intense that transcends, and makes me feel like I'm going to melt into a puddle on the floor.

God. Sex isn't even that great. I already know that.

I *had* to go have sex when I was sixteen. Partly because I spent a few years feeling like life was short and brutal and I needed to squeeze as much living in as I could, as soon as I could.

But shamefully, also so I could prove to myself there was no reason for Colt Campbell to have that kind of power over me. To prove that my crush was unreasonable. That the way that I felt when he walked into the room had nothing to do with reality. I did that.

The guy I lost my virginity to was a one-and-a-half-pump chump.

It was over so fast I barely felt it.

To be fair, we were both so young, it was both of our first times, and he was overexcited. It was better the next couple of times, at least in the sense that he lasted a bit longer. But I still didn't orgasm or anything.

I have had orgasms with partners since then, but it wasn't... It hasn't been... Nothing undeniable. Nothing world-shattering. Nothing life-altering.

But the feeling of Colt Campbell's hand on my hip is like a complete and total reimagining of everything I've ever believed my body could feel. Everything I've ever wanted, everything I've ever believed might be possible.

He's looking up at me, fire in his blue eyes, and I can't look away. Does he want me?

The thought is so horrible, so wonderful, so frightening, that I move away from him. Because I can't stand it, I can't process it.

"Careful," he says, his voice rough.

"Yeah. Fine."

"You're lecturing me on doing too much, but you're not really taking care of yourself."

"I have a lot to do. I'm just clumsy, I'm not negligent."

"You had a concussion."

"More than three weeks ago and I barely had any symptoms."

"Yeah. Sure. Right then, you didn't seem any steadier on your feet than I am. Makes me a little concerned for your safety."

I think he's actually being sincere, and not messing with me. But I do think he's also saying it because he wants to feel like he's taking care of me. Maybe that's where all the sincerity about my hard work in my schooling comes from. Trying to reposition this whole thing. Reposition himself, because I saw the total discomfort in his eyes when I had to help him down from the truck. I know this is killing him. But God damn, he just about killed me.

I'm gasping, my heart pounding so hard I'm sure that he can hear it. And if he can't hear that, then surely he can tell that I'm trying to suck in air like a fish that got tossed out of its bowl and onto the countertop.

I'm like a tragic, under-sexed guppy.

But then, so is he. That clarity rolls right to the front of my brain. He's trying to feel more like himself. He's stuck like this, and he feels diminished. Attraction... Having a woman want him, that's something he's familiar with. It's something that makes them feel good. And suddenly, I feel small.

Because he's never looked at me that way before. I've never seen fire like that in his eyes, and I know it's not really about me. It's about him. It's about the way that he feels about himself. It's about his need to feel like he's healing. Getting back to normal. Because God knows if he were out there in the arena tonight, collecting cheers from the crowd, he wouldn't be desperate for me.

He would have plenty of attention. Attention, that's a hell of a lot more desirable to him than mine.

All the heat inside of me is doused by that thought, and I turn away from him.

"Your mom invited us over tomorrow night."

"Okay."

"Since you're feeling so much better, that shouldn't be difficult."

"Yeah. I'm sure it won't be."

"I have a test that I have to go in person for. So I'm going to be driving to campus. And I won't be around."

"That's fine."

"Just... Just so you know."

"Okay."

"I'll see you tomorrow."

"Yeah. Okay."

I can tell that my abrupt departure is confusing to him. But I would rather have them stay confused and have him look at me for too long and know exactly what I'm feeling.

Because that would be one humiliation too many.

Chapter Nine

Colt

I was actually trying to be nice last night, but I managed to get under Allison's skin anyway. She was obviously mad at me when she left. And my palm was still burning from where I grabbed her hip.

God dammit. I don't need to be fixating on how pretty she is right now. That's one of those weird aberrations that has popped up a few times in the last few years, but nothing that I've been around long enough to let become a problem. I don't generally sit in rooms with her for this long, not without the buffer of Gentry, my mom, and Jim. It's just not something that usually happens.

Because of that, I am not generally left marinating in it.

But this has been a lot of Allison in a short amount of time.

And I'm more affected than I would like to be.

But then, that's a theme in my life right now. I'm more affected by fucking everything that I would like to be.

When I woke up this morning, my whole body hurt. That hurt hasn't gone away. I pound down a few extra strength painkillers – just the over-the-counter kind, not the intense ones, and tried to sit and watch TV. But I'm bored. I'm bored by everything. Before the season started, I was working on a project in the yard. And I'm half tempted to go see what I can get done now. I try to push that intrusive thought away. I'm supposed to be sitting still.

But the more I sit, the more I just stare at the wall, the more I see my own accident replaying, over and over again.

Fuck this.

I can feel my pain, I'm not on massive doses of opiates, I'm going to go do something, because I can't stand this. Not anymore.

I feel like I can do it. I feel like I can, and so I think I will.

I get up off the couch, and I open the back door, looking at where I have half my pavers laid down to make a little patio area. Part of the deal with me living here, essentially rent-free, is that I do lots of home improvement stuff for the property, so that when my mom puts it up for rent, it'll have better value. And I don't like that the project is half done.

I stared down at the pile of pavers. Quite a few of the stacks are tall, so I don't even have to bend down to pick them up. And clutching a paver up against the side of my crutch my fingers curled around it as I move from one side of the yard to the other isn't that hard. Bending down to put it in place, that's a different story. It's my damned ab muscles.

They got so torn up by that animal that I can feel my diminished core strength anytime I try to do something. But it's not terribly painful, it's just difficult. As long as I can make sure my leg stays stabilized. Then I'm good.

Though as my piles of pavers get shorter, bending to pick them up becomes more of a problem. The late afternoon sun is beating down on me, and I'm starting to feel a little bit lightheaded. I'm not sure how long it's been since I had water, and... Well, it was with my painkillers, which I think now happened hours ago.

But I'm making progress, and I'm much happier doing this than sitting on my ass. So I keep going.

I keep going until I'm lightheaded from how much everything is starting to hurt. It's deceptive, I think, how much extra weight the pavers are adding, or maybe it's just the extra back-and-forth, and even though I'm relying on my crutches, there's more weight than I realize being transferred to my injured leg.

I can feel my body telling me to stop. My head even tells me to stop, but there's something stubborn in my gut that keeps on going. There are only five left to put in place, and that stubborn part of me wants to finish it.

Because if I want to, I will.

Because that's the way I've always done things.

Until I pick up the last paver, and my crutch slips from under me, and I fall forward, my leg going behind me. "Fuck!"

I fall forward. And even though I'm able to catch myself with my arms, I don't entirely mitigate the impact.

I'm sweating, and not just from the heat. There are black dots swimming in front of my eyes. I'm losing consciousness. The pain is so excruciating. I roll over onto my back, breathing hard, my forearm over my eyes as my stomach cramps intensely and I lose consciousness altogether. Everything is blank. And then I open my eyes. It feels like it's been one extended blank. But I'm not alone when my eyes open. And that's my first clue that it's been a little longer than a single breath since I closed my eyes.

"What the hell are you doing?"

"I was finishing a project."

Allison is staring down at me like she wants to kill me. Or help me back up. "What's wrong? What are you hurt? Did you hit your head?"

She sounds frantic. And upset.

"I didn't hit my head. I just... I bent my leg weird, and it hurt. I also think I haven't had enough water today."

"We need to call your doctor."

"I don't need my doctor. I'm fine." I push myself up into a sitting position, and my head is swimming.

"Just let me get you some water."

She disappears into the house, and I am left to feel like a fucking tool. Because here I am, the God damned damsel in distress again, while she rushes off to save me, this time for myself. I let out a long, slow breath as I sit there, and she returns with a glass of water. The way she hands it to me expresses her deep disapproval of my behavior. And fine. Just fine.

"Sorry," I say. "But I was going nuts here doing nothing. I can't stand it."

"But you have to do nothing, you dumb ass. You just do. You're not Superman. I know that you feel like you are because your body used to do what you wanted it to do, but it's not now. And it's not a moral failure to have to heal, Colt. But it is really, really stupid to push yourself when you need to rest."

I hate that she's lecturing me. And I hate that I need one. I'm just pissed. I'm fucking pissed off. And I'm...

I'm tired of her yelling at me. I'm tired of her being right. I'm tired of...

With strength that comes from I don't even know where, I push myself up to my feet. And I barrel toward her, bracing myself on the side of the house as she backs up, our faces inches away. "I am not a child, and I don't need you to talk down to me." I'm breathing hard. "Yeah, this wasn't the best idea, but I'm fine. I'm not... I'm not broken, Allison." I can smell the scent of violets on her skin. And my whole body tightens. Everything inside of me roared at that soft, flowery smell.

"I could prove it to you," I whisper, my voice sounding rough. "That I'm not. I could still make you beg for me."

I don't know what the fuck has gotten into me that those words come out of my mouth, that I say them to my stepsister. Except I just know that the feeling inside of me is something desperate. I don't feel like myself. And I want to. I need to.

My heart is pounding so hard I can barely breathe. There's not a whole lot of forbidden fruit in my life. Hell, I can't say that I've ever really thought I wanted it. Right now, with her lips so close to mine, I can almost taste it, and her. She's the one woman I can't touch. I want to. God.

I feel like it might fix everything. I feel like –

"Don't."

Her words are firm and decisive. "Don't do this to me. If you need a pain pill, take a fucking pain pill, but I am not an opiate for your ego, Colt Campbell. I refuse to be. I won't be. I'm not going to make you feel better about yourself, or make you feel like you're whole. That isn't fair. That isn't fair of you to try and do this to me."

I rear back. "I'm not."

"You fucking are. You've never looked at me twice. Not ever, and then suddenly yesterday, today... Suddenly, now you want to kiss me? I'm your stepsister, you dumbass. And before that, I was your best friend's annoying little sister, and we both know that is the only way that you have ever looked at me. Ever. Don't try to pretend that now you magically see something in me. What you see is weakness in yourself, and you don't like it. What you see is your own mortality, and you want to feel something else instead, but I'm a person. I'm not a buckle bunny, I'm not some girl you can fuck while you're on the circuit and then forget about. You're going to have to see me almost every day for the rest of your life. Our parents are married. I am a giant consequence that you will struggle to be free of, so I would think better of it. If you can't think better of it because I deserve better than being used, at least think of how awkward Thanksgiving would be."

She slips away from me and goes into the house, slamming the glass door behind her.

"Fuck," I say. This backyard is soaking up more colorful language now that it's probably seen in its last hundred and fifty years of existence.

I really screwed up. I was not trying to hurt her. I wasn't trying to use her. But I can't deny that half of what's been driving me is this need to feel something. But I'm not using her in the way she means. I feel like she might be the answer. Her specifically.

Maybe.

She's right about Thanksgiving, though. But then, I have decent relationships with women I've slept with. There are a few women in town that I have ongoing things with. No animosity. No expectations, no nothing. It doesn't need to be contentious. But the problem is, I can't be all that articulate about my attraction to her, because it's not something I've given enough thought to. On purpose. The minute that I first felt attracted to her, I shut that shit down.

I'm not the kind of dark, tortured motherfucker who's just going to sit around thinking about how he wants his stepsister in a biblical fashion. It's just not my style. I don't do longing. I simply don't.

As soon as I started feeling that, I just cut it off. I'm good at that.

I take a deep breath. And I marvel at how many stupid things have happened in the last hour. It's kind of impressive.

I let out a breath, and I head into the house, because if there's one thing I'm not, it's a coward.

"Allison?"

"I'm here," she says. She pops out of the kitchen and stands there staring at me. "I'm not going to leave you here to die just because I'm mad at you."

"I'm sorry. You're right. About us. About the fact that it's not right. Because of our relationship. But I don't want you to think that the only reason it happened is because I feel bad about myself."

"Then why did it happen?"

"Because I've actually been in close proximity with you for too long. Because I... You're hot. That's just true. And I don't sit around dwelling on that. Okay?"

"Oh."

"I'm not so small that I have to try to make myself feel better by giving myself a pity fuck, okay?"

"That's... I believe you." She looks bothered by that. But hell, I'm bothered by it. It also galls me a little bit that there's an element of... It's not that. It's not. But I do feel a little bit small, and I can't say that I've ever felt that before in my life. I feel helpless. I don't want to be in my body, so I don't understand why anybody would want my body in them.

Jesus. I hate all this.

Above all else, I'm in a really bad place right now. And one thing I can't be doing is dragging Allison down here with me. There would be real consequences to that. There's a reason she's forbidden.

I wish that word didn't make my blood feel hotter. I wish my cock wasn't hard for the first time in fucking weeks.

"We can just forget it happened," she says. "I want to forget it happened."

"Yeah. We'll forget it."

"We have dinner at Cindy and Dad's tonight."

"Yeah. I know." Her voice is flat.

"So, we can't go... At each other's throats."

Well, that has a different connotation now.

This feels bad. Like the air around us has changed. And our mouths didn't even touch. What the hell would've happened if they had? We might've torn the space-time continuum. Might have caused the big one that Oregon's been waiting for all this time, the kind of cataclysmic earthquake that brings down everything around it, knocks out the power grid, and flattens whole buildings.

All because I lost my grip on who I am and what matters. I want to keep reassuring her. I want to make her feel better. I'm not in the business of hurting women's feelings. When I sleep with somebody, I want them to feel better about themselves when all is said and done. But I can't keep reassuring her, because there are bone fragments of lies in all the reassurance I want to give.

The truth is, things *have* changed.

I've changed.

My whole situation is upside down, and I can't guarantee that those slivers of bone aren't an even bigger deal than I think.

That they aren't more of a damaging half-truth that I'd like to believe.

How much of it is about me?

The truth is, I'm kind of selfish. I cover all that up by being nice to everybody. Smiling at everybody. I make that selfishness palatable. I'm going to try not to do that here.

"I need a shower."

"What if you pass out?"

"I'm not going to pass out."

"You hurt yourself. I really do think we should maybe go get your leg looked at."

"It doesn't hurt anymore. I swear, if I have any kind of lingering pain, I'll go get it looked at."

"Drink a glass of water."

There's a wall up between us, and that's fair. I drink a glass of water, and then I go to the shower. I know she's still not happy about it, but I have the bench, and I don't feel at all lightheaded. But the problem is, now I feel aware of better feelings in my body. More than just pain. As the water sluices over my skin, I think about her. About her lips. They're plump, the color of raspberries, and I can't recall ever wanting to taste something quite so much.

Am I that basic? So basic that something being out of reach grabs hold of me now because I'm bored? No. I don't think that's the case.

That's really shitty, if so.

But I'm getting hard thinking about her, and that makes me really mad, because I decided that I didn't want to feel it, so it should just be over.

I lost control of everything. Every aspect of my body seems to belong to some outside entity now. It's infuriating.

Absolutely infuriating.

I switch the water to cold, and grit my teeth together,

my hands braced on my thighs as it pounds down on my back. Penance. I'm not a big fan of penance. I'm not a martyr. Not at all. I don't like to be uncomfortable. I don't do resistance.

Maybe that's why I don't like forbidden. Normally.

If I were bigger into baseball, I could recite some stats. I start thinking about the NFL playoffs. And then I start thinking about my accident. That does it. Everything inside me shuts off quickly.

Unsurprisingly.

I get dressed in another pair of ruined Wranglers, and I think about how fucking absurd it would look if I didn't have the brace on. It's almost enough to make me laugh. But nothing much is funny right now. Still, the image of me with my whole leg out in a pair of jeans with a slit up the side is pretty funny. I'd look like a regular saloon girl at a much more progressive establishment than usually found in the wild west.

Hell. Maybe that'll be how I make my money after this. Some cowboy OnlyFans where I give people a good taste of hairy thigh.

That's a problem. I just can't figure out how much my life is actually going to change. I don't want to. Today was a sharp reminder that it has, though. I push it all away. Push it to the side. I need to put on a smile for dinner. I don't want my mom to be worried. I don't need Gentry to be worried.

Hell, I don't even want Lily to be worried.

My stepdad... He's always been proud of me. Of what I accomplished in the rodeo. It's gone a long way in healing some of the shit with my dad. What if I can't do anything anymore?

This is depressing.

I grab my black cowboy hat and put it on my head. Then I take hold of my crutches and walk out of the room.

Allison is sitting in that same chair she was in the other night. She's dressed in a white summer dress today. It's so strange, because I was a scant inch from her mouth, and I didn't notice what she was wearing, maybe because I was still dizzy from fainting. Fainting.

Damn.

Or maybe it's because I was dizzy from the violets.

"Ready?"

"You know," I say. "It's not my driving leg. I could probably drive."

"Yeah. The man who lost consciousness a few hours ago should drive."

"I'm fine now."

"Yeah. You're totally fine. You're doing great."

"Nobody asked for sarcasm, Allison."

"But you're gonna get it."

"I'm driving."

The thing is, she's not wrong, and I know that. I just don't want her to be right. But I get into the passenger seat of her car, which is in my driveway. When we get in, I realize I didn't ask her about her test.

"How did things go today?"

"Oh. Good. I mean, I don't know yet if I passed, but I've been doing okay with all of it."

"You want to be a nurse because of your mom, don't you?"

I knew her mom. I remember her, just vaguely. Often, she didn't feel very well when I would come over and hang out with Gentry. But she was nice, even while she was going through her treatments. She would have good days sometimes, and then she would make us snacks. She wore different wigs all the time, because she used to say that everyone knew her hair was gone anyway, so she wasn't trying to fool anyone, but she also didn't like going out bald either.

"Yeah," she says. She starts the car and pulls it out of the driveway. I guess I haven't earned any elaboration today. Fair enough. I wasn't my best self. I'm not my best self. Do I have a best self?

I'm usually a winner. Then I find my true North from that position. I figure out where I'm headed, what I want, and what other people think of me based on that. Now that I don't have it, I just kind of feel like a jackass.

It makes me question what I've ever done for anyone. Other than impress them. And what is that? What is it really? And what does it matter?

Nothing. Not a god damn thing.

Our parents' place is out of town, nestled near the base of the mountains. They've got a great spread. My stepdad's ranch is smaller than some around the area. There are some huge spreads in Gold Valley, including Dallas's family ranch, Get Out of Dodge.

He has certified organic grass-fed beef. He does good business selling to restaurants as far north as Seattle. There's a slightly different pace to this ranch than to a large operation, and I like it. Once he retires, I'd like to take over the family business. On my own property, of course. Of course, he's only just now fifty, so it'll be a while before he retires, but ideally, it'll be a while before I settle down after the rodeo.

Suddenly, the timeline all feels like a blur. And the future that I've always imagined for myself isn't stretching out in front of me like a wide flat road.

It's blank.

We don't talk for the entire car ride. But I'm pretty satisfied that we don't look like we want to tear each other apart. Or tear each other's clothes off.

I grit my teeth. That's a dumb thing to think about. It's a really dumb thing to think about.

Yes. She's beautiful. I noticed that a long time ago. But I don't need to let it fill me up now just because there's a void inside of me where the rodeo should be.

I can't do that to her. I can't do that to us, to the family.

She made it all very clear earlier today. She was assertive about it.

She doesn't want this.

And that's just fine.

Neither of us should want it.

Stepsiblings.

My thoughts are interrupted when we pull onto the dirt road that leads to our parents' place. She takes the dirt road a little bit quick, the tire slipping as she rounds the corners, but it's what I would do.

We've both driven this road so many times we could practically drive it with our eyes closed. Her little car doesn't have the traction my truck does, though.

"Speed demon," I say.

"Like you aren't," she says.

I have nothing to say to that. She pulls up next to Gentry's truck, right there in front of the house.

"I don't need help," I say, opening the door and managing to get my crutch planted in the gravel driveway.

"Don't be stubborn," she says.

"I'm stubborn. Deal with it." I manage to maneuver myself out of the truck without having an incident. I'm grateful for that. I don't need any more incidents today. I don't need any more incidents ever. I've maxed out on those. For the rest of my life.

"You don't have to do that."

"Yeah. I have to do it." I guess she means that I don't have to do it by myself. I don't have to put distance between us. The answer to both of those things is that I do. She doesn't get to make proclamations. I'm the one who screwed up earlier. I'm the one who hurt her. I don't want to do that. Not again.

I take the stairs up the front porch slowly, but it's not impossible. It's just methodical. She's standing behind me. Like if I fall backward, we can trust fall or something. I don't say anything. I just grit my teeth and get myself up to the front door. My mom doesn't even let me ring the doorbell before she's flying halfway out onto the porch. "I'm so glad that you felt well enough to come tonight."

I wrap her in my arms as best I can while bracing myself on the crutches. "Of course. Thanks for inviting me."

"You know you're welcome here anytime. But I figure that you needed to rest a little bit at home first."

"Yeah. Probably." Except the rest makes my skin itch and makes me feel like my brain's on fire, but that's fine.

"How's he doing?"

My mom directs this question to Allison. I wait for her to tattle on me.

"Great. I mean, you know how he is. He wants to take things a little faster than he should, but other than that, he seems to be doing great. That's my professional medical opinion."

She's being too nice. I don't like it.

But she goes into the house, and my mom does too, so I just follow them in.

Gentry and Lily are sitting in the dining room already talking to Jim.

"Glad they let you off to come have dinner," I say to my stepbrother.

"Yeah. We got the Trigger Fire 90% lined. Everything's going great. I'm going to get moved to a different location in a couple of days, but I'll have some time off until then."

"Yeah, we're both getting sent to California," Lily says.

Lily is one of the few women that I've ever known to fight wildland fires. She takes the job seriously, but then, she's always been one of us. I half expected her to take up bull riding when Dallas and I started it, but she went with the firefighting.

Probably because Gentry is the person that she's really attached to. Not that she's ever said that. Not that it's something we ever speak about. But it's apparent to me.

"Well, great that you guys get to drive down together."

"Yeah."

"Maybe I'll do some firefighting after I'm done with the rodeo," I say, sitting down at the table.

"Excuse me?"

My mom walks into the room holding a basket of bread.

"Just planning for the future, mom."

"Could you give me a break? Because I would like that, Colt. What if you became an accountant?"

Lily snorts, and Gentry smiles and looks up at my mom. "Do you know *accountant* is a chronically online euphemism for something else?"

"No," Cindy says. "For what?"

"For a sex worker," says Lily.

My mom rolls her eyes. "Oh, please."

"I was thinking about that earlier," I say. "I could start a rodeo cowboy page."

"If you do that, you have to not tell me," my mom says.

"No, I'll definitely tell you."

"You're trouble," she says, swatting me on the shoulder, and one of the very few places I'm not injured.

Allison isn't in the room., And I'm wondering where she went. But I don't ask. Mom leaves and comes back in with a pan of meatloaf and a bowl of mashed potatoes, followed by a giant bowl of green salad. Allison appears after everyone starts taking their plates out of the pile at the center of the table.

She sits down at the table at the furthest seat away from me. Is that what she was waiting for? A way to sit as far from me as possible without it being obvious? Like she just took the last seat.

Though she did take the last seat, and there's no way she planned that, I guess. But still.

"How's school?" Gentry jabbed his fork toward Allison, and then she proceeds to give him the same rundown she gave me earlier.

I'm not used to spending so much time with her. Normally, this would be news to me. But I feel like I've been on the interior of her life now for the past couple of days. A couple days that feel a hell of a lot longer than they actually were.

But that's part of the time warp of this injury. It feels both like no time has passed at all since that night at the rodeo, and like I've lived an entirely new lifetime.

And yet, here I am, surrounded by my family. That's a gift. I wonder how many people are lucky enough to have a family as nice as this? Here we are, all sitting around the table. There's no tension. There's no weirdness. It's a blended family, and yet we all get along. Gentry and I are practically best friends. My mom gets along with both step-kids, and Jim is the father I never had. It couldn't be more important.

The only tension that has ever existed has been between Allison and me, and that's just normal.

You. It's normal.

At least mostly was until today.

But this is the reminder for why we can't do this. The reminder for why from the very first moment I ever felt attracted to her I decided that I had to shut it off.

And I need to shut it off now, too.

Because this family is what matters. It means everything to me. And now that I don't have the rodeo, this is what I have. It's all I have.

She looks up, right at that moment, and our eyes clash.

My stomach feels like she reached through that stitched-up wound in my side and wrapped her hand around it.

I can't not see that moment earlier today. Where I was staring at her mouth, looking at it and realizing that I wanted to devour it. That I want to devour her.

She looks away, down at her food, driving her fork through her mashed potatoes, and I have a feeling she's imagining driving that fork through my hand.

Joke's on her. It wouldn't hurt as bad as getting gored by a bull. As much as I know she would like for it to. And still, I'm having trouble taking my eyes off of her.

"Does anybody want dessert?"

My stepdad makes a mean pie. My mom made dinner, but I guarantee he's the architect of whatever masterpiece is coming out last.

Everyone agrees to dessert – obviously – and Jim gets up from the table and heads into the kitchen, coming back with two beautiful pies. "Huckleberry and blackberry, berries picked by me."

See, this is what I mean. Idyllic. Everyone gets heaping helpings of pie, and vanilla ice cream to go with. And I forget for a little bit that everything is shit. Honestly. That's how good Jim's pies are. That's how good it is to be here with my family. That's how normal it is. How wonderful it is.

"You and Dad should go sit," Allison says. "I'll do the dishes."

"We can help," Lily says.

Though, it's obvious that they're wrecked from work.

Allison sees it immediately. "No. The firefighters should go home and rest. Seriously. Until I start my clinical rotations, I'm not nearly as exhausted as anybody here."

I think she's downplaying. I'm noticing that she does that quite a bit. I haven't really noticed that before. I don't get why she does that.

I wouldn't think that she admires what I do so much, maybe what Gentry does. He actually helps people. Makes a difference.

"I don't want to leave you with everything," Gentry says.

"I'm good," she says, making a shoeing motion. "Seriously. Get out of here."

I wait until Lily and Gentry are gone, and then I push myself into a standing position.

Allison whirls around toward me. "No. You're not going to–"

"Allison," I say. "I can dry some dishes. I'm not that bad off."

I can see that she's really weighing arguing with me. But also the moment that she decides it's not worth it.

Smart girl.

Although, as we head into the kitchen together, Allison with a stack of plates nearly scraped clean of pie residue, I realize that it might not have been the best idea.

Because here we are by ourselves in the kitchen. I think we must've done the dishes together a hundred times, though. And I've never given any thought to it.

In fact, I remember very clearly her being about thirteen and angry that she was being made to clean up and Gentry and I harassing her by snapping dishtowels in her direction.

She got mad, and even almost started crying. Yeah, it kind of makes sense why she doesn't like me. I was annoying, and I was sort of intrigued by the idea of being a brother. I was by myself all my life. And then I got Gentry. Then I got her. So teasing her seemed like the right thing to do, and she was soft and easy to get a rise out of.

I realize now, though, that it probably wasn't the most gallant move.

"All right. Let's set up an assembly line."

"I don't really need an assembly line. I'm perfectly capable of doing the dishes. You're the one who insisted that you help."

"Yeah. I'm insisting."

She rolls her eyes, and begins filling the sink with water. We have a dishwasher. It's just one of those things. My mom will put pots and baking dishes and things like that in, but she doesn't want to run it for dinner dishes. And so we've always done hand washing at the end of a meal. It's possible that she was doing it back then so that we could build relationships. And also quite possible that she still does it now so that she doesn't have to admit that. That seems like it would be pretty on brand for my mom.

I smile and grab my dish towel.

"What?"

"Oh. I was just thinking about the possibility that my mom makes us hand-wash to force us all to get along."

"I never thought of that."

"Did you do dishes like this before Jim and Mom got married?"

"I think Dad usually did them. I don't know. Your mom is the one who made us start doing some chores. I think my dad felt so... I don't know. I don't think he ever thought he could make us do things."

She doesn't have to say it. I get it. He felt guilty. Gentry and Allison lost their mom.

"But then, my dad did a lot of the housework. While my mom was sick. They used to do it together. But mostly it was him doing it." I noticed that her eyes were glistening. I imagine all this brings lost like that closer to the surface. Not that I think I matter in the way that her mom does. I just think that it's probably hard to be in hospitals, looking at somebody that you know being sick, injured, and not think about other times that's happened to you. I totally get why she's going into nursing. I totally get why it's a tribute to her mom. But I also wonder why she's putting herself through something traumatizing like that on purpose.

"Isn't going to be hard for you? Being in the hospital all the time?"

She looks at me. "I never forget that she's gone. It's just sort of part of my life. She was so great. I wish that you had known her a little bit better. But she made sure that we sat together, had tea parties. In the summer, when she would go get her infusions, I would go with her. I would sit there in the cancer center, and I would watch her knit. I didn't start knitting until recently. It made me wish that she could see it. It made me wish that I had known how to do it then, so we could've done it together. I guess my childhood could be full of bad memories. But she was sick off and on for nine years. It was almost my entire life. I barely knew my mom without cancer. And so, the times that I spent with her in hospitals have to be part of my good memories too. I have good memories of her when she was sick. Because it was just part of all the time that I got to have with her. I hate that she was sick. I hate the illness, don't get me wrong. But I don't want to let any precious moment of time that I had with my mother become something that I push away because it's too difficult."

She sticks her hand into the sink and tests the temperature of the water. And then she puts the dishes down into the soapy liquid. "Maybe that's why I gravitated toward taking work at the hospital. Not just so I can make a difference to people who are sick, but because... It's just part of my life."

"You're pretty fucking amazing," I say, looking at her with a sense of all filling me. "Do you know that?"

She looks up at me, shock on her beautiful face.

Like she's surprised I'm complimenting her. Or maybe surprised that I am in light of the whole rest of today, which was kind of a shit show.

"I don't become amazing. I'm just shaped by the things that I went through."

"I feel traumatized by the hospital, and I was only there for a few weeks."

She snorts. "Well, if you had asked my mom how she felt about the hospital she might've had a different answer for you. I think it's different when you're the one who's sick. I think it's different for a lot of people. We all handle the things that life throws at us in different ways. This is how I handled it. It's not better. Or stronger. It's just my way of coping."

"My way of coping is to try to do things that I'm not supposed to do," I say.

Her expression goes flat. "That's not going to fly with me."

I smile. She starts scrubbing the dishes, then passes them over to me to rinse and dry. We create a seamless assembly line, and I don't even react when her fingertips brush mine. I don't need to react. It's casual. It's the same kind of stuff we've always done. It's part of this very normal evening that we spent at our parents' house.

"Did your mom always make you wash dishes before our parents got married?"

"Right. You never came over to our house, did you?"

"No. I only ever saw you when you came over here."

"Yeah. Of course. That never occurred to me. Yes. My mom was really strict. I had to do chores even when Gentry came over to visit."

"I can't even imagine that. Your mom has never been all that strict as long as I've known her."

"Yeah. We've talked about it since. She was just really afraid. Me growing up without a dad. Plus, my dad..." Oh God dammit. I didn't mean to get into this territory. I never talk about him. There's really no reason to, because he's not around.

"What about your dad?"

"Because he's irresponsible. And so I think my mom really felt like she had to overcompensate. Not just because I didn't have a male role model in my life, but because the man that I'm related to is not the best."

"That makes sense. Kind of. It's not your fault, though. It's not like you chose your dad."

"Well. No. But in fairness, he didn't choose me either. Something he made very clear over the years."

"Have you met him?"

I nod slowly. "Yeah. I've met him. He sort of came to one of my birthday parties one time. And I went to see him ride in the rodeo."

"Is that why you became a bull rider?"

"Yes and no," I say slowly. "I wanted to do it, because I liked it. But there was part of me that thought... *This is the only thing you care about, and I can do it too. You don't think I'm special, but I can do the thing that you think makes you special, and I'll be better at it.* Of course, the problem with narcissists is that they don't really notice when you mount campaigns like that. Because it would require them to pay the tiniest bit of attention to someone who isn't them. And that doesn't happen."

She slows her movements, hands buried in the sink. "Wow. That is so... Deeply unsatisfying."

"You're telling me. I was expecting to show up to the rodeo and be like: Hey, Dad, look at me." I shake my head. "He didn't even look twice at me. All the times we passed each other at events – he wasn't riding anymore then but he used to make appearances and shit, and he just looked through me half the time. Or worse, would say hi casually like I was a fan. He just doesn't care. That's the thing. He doesn't care. He doesn't care about anybody but himself, and he never has. I've accepted it now. It doesn't add anything to my life to think about him. Not ever. So I just don't." I don't consider my thinking about him when I was hopped up on pain pills to be me breaking that practice. It doesn't count.

"At least my mom didn't *choose* to leave."

"I guess. But honestly, that's one of the things that

makes me even matter. Your mom was great. She should still be here. My dad sucks. He should've had my accident. But no. He's walking around on two good legs with absolutely no good scruples."

She wrinkled her nose. "You think you have half-siblings?"

"I can't imagine that I don't. I'm sure if I uploaded my DNA to one of those websites it would go crazy."

"Sarah says that she won't do that for that reason."

I nod. "I mean, I haven't done it for a reason. I can't say that I especially want to meet a whole bunch of other people who are related to my dad. Not given everything I know about him."

"But maybe they're like you."

"Maybe. Maybe my dad had really good taste in women. And all of them made us into better people than he is. I'd like to think that's true."

Then I think about my behavior earlier, and I realize that Allison might think the idea that I'm a good person is sort of up for debate at this point. "I mean, I'm marginally better than my dad," I add.

"You're better than your dad," she says, handing me the last plate. "Don't... Don't do that."

"What?"

"You've been doing this whole guilt and sorrow thing, and I don't like it. I'd rather you just be yourself. You're annoying, you're cocky, you're a pain in the butt, but at least it's normal. I don't..."

She takes her hands out of the sink water and brushes them against her jeans, and then she turns away from me. Quickly.

I reach out and grab her by the arm, turning her toward me, and too late, I realize my mistake. I was focused on my guilt, not how I needed to watch myself around her. And now here we are, squaring off again, facing each other. And my heart is pounding hard. Just like it did out in the yard earlier.

"Allison," I say. "What if... What if this is normal for me now? What if there's no more of that guy that I used to be."

She swallows hard, I can see it. "I don't think that's true. I'm sure that you'll be back to normal."

"I'm not sure that I want to," I say. I don't know anything. That's the problem. My memories of getting thrown off the bull are terrible. I want to get back to my life, but I also don't want to get back to it. I don't want to be changed by this, but I know I have been.

"You kind of have to be affected by near-death experiences, don't you?"

"You don't have to do anything that you don't want."

"I want... I want to be more like you. I want to take the bad things and make them into good things."

"Colt," she whispers. "You've always been the best one. The one that everybody's drawn to. You're the one that everybody loves. You know that."

"I don't know if that's true." I reach out then, and without thinking, I drag my thumb over her cheekbone. It's like an electric shock, my skin against hers. She's touched me quite a bit over the last few weeks. Assisting me. Helping me out. But like my hand on her hip last night, this is different. It just feels different.

"Don't," she says.

"You said that already."

"You're not listening."

"I have a listening problem."

She turns away from me, and it's like my sanity returns to me in a rush. I was just thinking about how this couldn't happen. About how important the family is. The family. Fuck. She's my family.

My stepsister. Maybe we've never been close like that, maybe our relationship was shaped by those years when we didn't live together, but that's the reality of it now.

We come to this house for dinner. We have holidays here. Her dad makes pie.

I want to be him after I retire. I don't want to be my dad.

I know my mom worried a lot about that when I went into the rodeo. She thought I was chasing my dad's shadow, in all the worst ways, but I'm not. I never have been, not that way.

I want to be Jim. He's the man that I look up to. He's my father.

And he's also Allison's father, so that makes *this* impossible.

"Here's what I think," she says. "I think that you're going to heal up just fine. You're going to go back to the rodeo, and you're going to feel really silly that you ever opened this door between us."

"Door?"

"This door," she says, whirling back around and gesturing between the two of us. "This door. I've kept it close. I piled all the furniture in front of it. To make sure that it stayed that way. But you don't know that, because you didn't notice. Now you're noticing because you're sitting still. But that's the only reason. You're going to go back to your life. You can go back to your life and–"

"It's on Peacock." I hear my mom's voice growing closer, shouting toward Jim, I assume.

"I don't think it is," he calls back.

And then, there she is, standing in the same room as us

and all of our tension, reminding me why I'm an idiot, as if I hadn't already realized that.

"Everything okay?"

"Fine," I say.

"Yeah. We just finished." Allison goes back to the sink and reaches her hand into the water, draining it aggressively. "So now will just go. We'll just go home." I mean... I'll take him home."

"Okay," my mom says, looking between us, and if she has a question, she doesn't ask it.

That's one of the things I like about my mom.

"We're just trying to find something to watch. It used to be that all the streaming services were great. Now it's like having cable and Blockbuster rolled into one. Too much content, all divided up, and you can't find a single thing."

"The trials and travails of technology," I say.

She gives me side eye, and I deserve it. But I'm ready to get out of here.

I head toward the living room as quickly as I can, which isn't that quick. So I know that Allison is going to catch up to me. "Good night, Jim," I say. "Thanks for the pie."

"Yeah. Sure."

"Bye, Dad," Allison says.

"Bye, Sprite."

"Come for dinner again in a couple of days," Cindy calls.

"Yeah," Allison says. "Definitely. I mean, I'm sure Colt will be driving himself soon."

"Yeah. Probably."

"Don't push it," my mom says.

"I wouldn't dream of it."

We walk out onto the front porch, and she closes the door behind me.

"Thanks for not ratting me out." I don't even know which thing I mean.

"Yeah. Well. There are certain conversations that I don't want to have." That could apply to multiple things. It takes me forever to get down the stairs. But I don't let Allison help me. To be fair, she doesn't offer. But I think it's because she knows that I'm going to say no.

And then, we are shut in the small space in her car, and nothing is better.

"You're important to me," I say, once we're back on the main road. "I swear to God, I'm not doing anything."

"I'm important to you?"

"Yes. Our family is important. You're right. I can't be disrupting Thanksgivings."

"Oh. So I'm not important. I'm just a block in your Jenga tower."

"That's not what I'm saying."

"Yeah. It is what you're saying, Colt. But that's fair. You've had enough blocks taken out of the tower, haven't you? So, of course, you can't bear to have one more removed. But it's not about me. It's about you."

I think about the desire that I felt for her earlier. About the way that it built when I touched her cheek earlier. She pulls us into the driveway of my house, and at that point, I snap. "No, Allison. If it were about me, I'd have kissed you. And trust me, if I did that, pretty soon you'd be screaming my name and coming so hard we'd both forget why this is a bad idea."

I don't wait for her to help me out. I get out of the car, and I go straight to the house by myself.

I slam the door shut behind me, and if she tries to follow, I don't know.

Chapter Ten

Allison

I wake up feeling...uneasy. Maybe that isn't the right word. Colt leaving me in the car after he said that echoes in my head. It kept me awake last night. I couldn't sleep. I just kept hearing that angry, rough promise he made before he stormed into the house.

The trouble is, I believe it. The trouble is, I know that I had to rush out and have sex so that I wouldn't be wondering about him. The trouble is... Talking to Sarah makes me suspect that my worst fear is true. That with Colt it would be good. It would be *great*.

I press my fists into my eyeballs.

The truth is, I should move. For the last year of school, when I'm doing my rotations in the hospital, I would be much happier if I weren't living in Gold Valley. I would have more time to sleep, and I would spend less time commuting. And I wouldn't be so close to him.

I know exactly where this is leading me.

I get out of bed, and I strip my clothes off. I stalk to my shower and I turn the water on. I let the warm water beat down on me. And I wonder if I'm really considering...

The trouble is, I've been haunted by this for years. This is new for him. I know it is. He can say whatever he wants about how this isn't about where he's at emotionally right now, but it is. The idea that I could help him stop feeling like less of a man... Oh, that gets me in ways I don't like.

I was devastated the first time. I was devastated when he looked at me with that desire in his eyes and I realized it was only about his desire to feel whole. I reacted badly, and I had a good reason for it. But now I've been sitting with it for a good twelve hours. Well, more than that. In the kitchen last night, it's like I was a teenager again. It was like all those fluttery feelings rose up inside of me. And when we talk, I actually do like him. I only don't like him because I'm always desperately trying to put this wall between us.

What if I didn't? What if I just stop trying? What if we stop trying? What if... What if I can help him and he can show me how good sex is, and then I leave? Around the time he starts to feel better. I'll move away, and I won't have to deal with him. I won't have to deal with the consequences. It's almost the perfect crime.

My heart is pounding hard. Damn. At 7 AM. I really need to calm down.

But I can't. Because my body feels like it's on fire. Because I feel like I've finally come to a conclusion. I feel like I've finally shaken off the stagnation that has been dogging me.

Has it only been days since he got out of the hospital? It feels like months. It feels like so many things have changed fundamentally, but all those changes have been inside of me. Between us.

Barely spoken. We were talking around all of it until last night, right before he went into the house. All I need to know is if he wants me. If he wants me, I don't actually care why.

My nipples are hard, and I feel myself getting wet between my thighs.

I've had sex before.

Sex doesn't have to ruin everything. It barely even changes anything.

And the truth is, Colt has sex with tons of women, all the time. I'm quite certain that he runs into women he's slept with in town all the time. And it doesn't matter. It's fine.

It's totally okay that he's slept with them before, and they still see each other in town.

I mean, I still live in town with my ex-boyfriends. I really rarely think about them. When I run into them, it doesn't even feel awkward.

It's just that I've let the thing with Colt become so big. That's the real issue.

I built it up into something that it can't possibly live up to. And I sort of transposed the feelings that I had for him when I was a teenage girl onto the feelings that I might have for him as an adult woman. Why have this unresolved lust? Unresolved lust isn't love. It's not even a crush. I want him. And I think there's something fundamental about that.

He was my sexual awakening in so many ways.

The first man I ever fantasized about. They were innocent fantasies at first, of course.

I thought about kissing him. And then when I got older, I thought about a whole lot more.

He was the first human I had those concrete thoughts

about. He drove me straight into the bed of a very underskilled teenage boy.

But that's the problem, the idea of Colt still has so much cachet.

And what if I just found out? And what if we didn't let it ruin anything? Because he's right. Our family is so important. I let all this hurt me because I interpreted it in a negative way. The thing about Colt is that he never means anything in a bad way. He's kind of an ass, but he's never being mean. I'm the one who's prickly and difficult and always throws spikes down on the road in between us.

It doesn't have to be that way. I can change. I shut the water off. This is what men do when they talk themselves into having affairs? They just start telling themselves pretty stories that they polish and shine until the outcome is that they can excuse themselves to have the sex that they want, no matter how destructive it might be.

Maybe. I shut that moment of self-awareness away. I don't want self-awareness.

I want to scream his name.

Yeah. I am probably hallucinating. Half-asleep still. I should probably drink some coffee before I follow this train of thought. But instead, I pull on a pair of sweats and a hoodie, no underwear underneath either of them, and I walk out of my house, down the sidewalk toward Colt's house.

And with a little bit of guilt, I use my key on his front door and push it open. "Colt?"

I hear him walking down the hall. "Allison?"

He's wearing a pair of black boxer briefs, nothing else. Well, his brace. Oh. I wonder how that's going to be. Well. I can be on top. That's fine. I know what I'm doing. Thank

God I'm not a virgin. Thank God I have some experience to bring to the table.

Though I have a feeling if our experience was represented by M&Ms, his would be a bowl to my sad fun-size bag.

"Is everything okay? Something going on with mom?"

"It's me. I..."

And then I move forward, he's on his crutches, he's braced against the wall, I close the distance between us and wrap my arm around his neck. Stretch up on my toes, and I kiss him.

He grunts, releasing hold on one of his crutches as he braces his hand on my lower back.

His mouth is hot and sure on mine. He's shocked for a moment, but it doesn't take very long for him to get into the rhythm of things. And oh. My. God.

I've never really been kissed before. Not like this. Every pass of his tongue over mine is expert. He knows how to change the rhythm. How to command a response from me. I can't even fully explain it.

It's like he's a surgeon, expertly targeting the exact part of my body he wants to with each pass of his tongue. I can feel it, between my thighs, it makes my heart beat faster. I feel it as my nipples get tight, my breasts feeling heavy. He's just kissing me. He has one hand on me, still and steady on my lower back.

But it's like he's touching me all over. Like he's creating a whole symphony in my body and he's not even operating at full capacity. He's barely even trying.

It's enough to make me want to run away. Because this is everything I've ever been afraid to fantasize about. This was my deepest fear. That there was something with him that I was never going to be able to find with anyone else.

And that if I couldn't have it with him, I would never have it. Not with anyone.

Maybe we'll never have it again.

Or maybe this is the learning experience I need.

That same voice that drove me here pops up now. But right as I'm about to encourage myself forward, he breaks the kiss.

"Are you fucking kidding me?"

"What?"

"After... What's happening?"

"I was thinking."

"No. I don't believe that you were thinking. This is not thinking behavior."

This is crazy. I know that it is. But I don't want to stop. Besides, this isn't one day, one comment in the making. This is a lifetime full of fantasies building up to this one moment. This one incredible moment.

"I think we can help each other," I say.

"Help?"

He sounds out of breath. Horny, like I am. And I can tell that he's ready to make the same bargain with reality that I already did.

Whatever lie you have to tell yourself in order to get some. I know I'm ready.

"You want to... You want to get your groove back. And I... had some really disappointing sex."

"Excuse me?"

"I've had some really disappointing sex."

"Yeah, sorry, I did. The first time. I just don't quite know what to say to that."

"I feel like the sex between us wouldn't be disappointing."

He lifts a brow. "Oh. It wouldn't be. But this seems to

have come out of nowhere, and yesterday you were ticked off at the idea of me using you. So I need to know exactly what change." He grabs my hips, and sets me back a pace. "What changed, sweetheart?"

"I..." I'm short-circuiting because he called me sweetheart. Honestly, he probably calls every woman he touches that. Every woman who isn't related to him. I should probably be offended. I should probably take it as him minimizing me. Minimizing us. But I don't. I don't, because I find it hot, and I'm that basic. Oh God, I'm so basic.

But I'm willing to just basic bitch my way to multiple orgasms.

I'm willing to let all of reality slide. This is what I've always been afraid of. Honestly. This is why I've always kept that metaphorical furniture piled up against the door. I was afraid that if it cracked, even a little bit, I would be charging through it uninvited.

Here I am, doing just that. My resistance is nothing. My desire is everything.

"I..." Am I going to do this? Am I going to debase myself?

"Nothing has changed," I say.

Yes. I am. I'm doing this. I'm jumping right in. "I've wanted this for a long time. You. Me. Sex."

"You... You're kidding me." He looks shocked. Shook. He looks like he has no idea what I'm talking about. And I feel... Proud of my younger self? I guess that's weird. I feel proud of my younger self because she managed to hide it. She kept her pride. She did what needed to be done. Because apparently he's not completely aware of my longstanding feelings for him. So I guess there's that.

"Yeah. I wanted you before our parents got married. I had a crush on you. And then you moved in, and it got worse, and that's why I'm mean to you. Because I want to fuck you."

"Did you just... Did you just gender swap picking on somebody because you like them?"

"Yes. I like to think that it's been a great act of feminism on my part."

"Well. I guess so." He looks like he doesn't know what to say, and I'm almost amused that I've rendered Colt Campbell speechless. He's not the kind of man to be speechless. I have a feeling that when it comes to women, he always knows what to say. Always knows how to act. Always knows exactly what's happening next. I've managed to disrupt that. To throw him off. Cheers to me.

"It worked. We've managed to have a perfectly... Appropriate relationship for a lot of years. And I never jumped you."

"Until today."

"Until today. I know it's a bad idea. Except I feel like it doesn't have to be. Not if we are on the same page."

"No one can ever know," he says.

I laugh. Loud. Way too loud. It echoes in the room. "Yeah, no. No one can ever know. If they found out... I think we can handle this. I do. But I think that everybody else would lose their ever-loving minds. It's a small town. Can you even imagine?"

He shakes his head. "No. That would be something that follows us both, and I don't think either of us wants that."

"But you want me. Right now."

He nods. Slowly. I could ask him when that changed. I could ask why. I just don't think it's going to help me. I don't think it's going to benefit anything for me to have the full rundown of everything going on inside of him. I want my fantasy. And part of this has been deciding that I don't need it to be his.

There. I can feel something inside of me unburdened. Lighten. Float away.

I don't need this to be his fantasy. It just needs to be mine. This isn't going to be forever. No one can ever know that we're doing this. Only us. It's our secret. Our dirty, messed-up secret.

And whatever he's getting out of it, that's his business. Whatever I'm getting out of it, it's mine. "Disappointing sex?"

He moves closer to me. "Very."

"My leg is not... I don't know exactly how..."

"I don't think it's good to be disappointing."

"Oh, I've never disappointed anyone. My tongue works just fine."

I shiver.

"Oh."

I struggle, though, with understanding how he's gone from wherever he's normally at with me to being willing to lick me in intimate places. But then I see the fire banked in his eyes, and I decide I don't really care. I don't need the play-by-play. I'm going to keep telling myself that. So that I don't pull myself out of the moment. I've had a lot of disappointing sex, and part of the problem is me. I can never really lose myself in it. I'm an overthinker. I always have been.

Life has given me a lot of reasons to overthink. A mom with a long-term illness, which had me constantly analyzing every sign and symptom that I thought I might see in her when she was in between scans. Then my teenage crush moved into my house. Looking for signs and portents is sort of my thing.

But I don't want to overthink now. The whole reason that I walked through all of this in my head before I came over was so that I didn't do that. So that I could just let go.

"You really want to... You want to do that to me?"

"Come here," he says.

He takes my hand and, on his crutches, goes to sit down on the couch, leading me along with him. He sits, and then, without warning, pulls me on top of him while he lets his crutches fall. I'm straddling him, one thigh on either side of his. I can feel the hard ridge of his cock between my legs. Oh God. I'm dying. I'm dying in the very best way.

"I want you," he says. "You're beautiful."

I search his face, looking for something, something that feels specific to me. To this moment.

He's so familiar. *Colt*. I've seen his face change over the years.

From a boy who I thought was cute, growing more angular, becoming a man that I thought was beautiful. He's been my brother's friend, my idol, my crush, my stepbrother. My adversary.

My charge. My patient.

And now he's my ticket to pleasure. We're close, so close, our bodies pressed together, and what really stuns me is just how natural the progression feels. How right it is. How much it's not weird, even though it should be.

I lift my hand, and I skim my thumb over his lower lip, over the whiskers on his chin, along the line of his jaw. He's so beautiful.

Forbidden. This was the one thing I wasn't supposed to do. I wasn't supposed to do this. I wasn't supposed to show my hand.

But I have.

"Kiss me," he says.

He's leaving it up to me. His hand is pressed against my lower back, and his other rests at his side. He's waiting for me to take it there.

I bite my lower lip, and I look at him. Then I lift both my hands so that they're bracketing his face. I want to savor this moment. I jumped in with both feet. He's my stepbrother. My lifelong fantasy. I'm straddling his lap. I've got his hard cock pressed up against me. I'm going to savor this moment. I'm going to linger in it. Let it take a little bit of time. Because it's already taken ten years. So I might as well take this breath. Take these few ticks of the clock. To really let it sink in that it's him. Finally.

I lean in, press my mouth to his, just slightly. Then I move to the left corner of his lips, kissing him across the width of that mouth. Then moving back to the center again and kissing him a bit more deeply. He groans beneath me, two hands going to my hips as he pulls me down hard against him. And I arch my back in pleasure.

I think it's going to happen here. Right here on the couch. But this is perfect. The ideal position given his leg.

"I haven't wanted this. For weeks now. Haven't even had fantasies. Not until you. You got under my skin, Allison."

My name on his lips is enough. Tortured, broken. My name on his lips is enough to make me feel special. It's enough to make me feel wanted in this moment. I'll take it. I'll cling to it and let it make this feel real. Make it feel right. Because I needed. I need him.

And I'm going to claim him.

I lean back and grip the hem of my hoodie. Pull it off. I don't have anything on underneath, and my breasts are bare, right in his face. It was like that when he gripped my hip when I tripped in the kitchen. But this time, there's no fabric between us. I can see him take a breath, hold it. A muscle in his jaw jumps like he's tense. Trying to hold himself together. Trying to keep steady. Then his hands move up my bareback, fingertips tracing the line of my spine as he pushes me forward, bringing my nipples up against his lips. His tongue darts out, tasting the tip of one, and my whole body shudders.

Oh God.

He's going to kill me. I've never felt anything like this before. And I'm going to be so mad when I have to tell Sarah that I know now that sex can actually be amazing.

No. I can't tell her. I can't tell anyone. No one can ever know that this happened between me and Colt. I have to remember that.

It would make the town dynamics so weird. Our family dynamic is so weird. We just can't.

But... I can't not have him. I can't.

Right as I think that, he parts his lips, blows against my nipple, turning it into a point so hard it could cut glass. Then he draws it deep into his mouth, sucking hard. Men have done this to me before. But it hasn't felt like this. It's that indefinable chemistry that feels so unfair. Because I didn't ask to feel this for Colt. But I do. It's beyond me.

"You're just perfect," he groans. He presses a hot kiss to the valley between my breasts before moving his attention to the next one. Sucking my other nipple deep into his mouth, and the sound he makes – one of pure helplessness – lets me know that I'm not alone in this. That he felt just the same way I do. That he is helpless in the face of this chemistry. What does it matter when it happened for him? He feels it. He didn't think about sex since the accident, and now he wants me. So I don't care if he ever wanted me before. I don't care how many women he's been with. I don't care about anything but how good this feels. As long as the chemistry exploding between us is mutual, that's all that matters.

He moves his hands up, cups my breasts, thumbs skimming over my damp nipples. Then he pinches me lightly. I feel an answering pulse at the center of my core. He moves his hands down my midsection, pushes one down beneath the waistband of my sweats. Finds me bare underneath. He growls when his fingertip makes contact with my core. I'm so wet. I know he feels that. He moves deeper, touches me more intimately. One finger pushing inside of me with ease because I'm just so ready for him.

It's all moving too fast, and not fast enough. I want it to go on forever. I want him inside me now. I wish that I could draw it out. Part of me does. I wish I could be on the precipice of having not quite done this for just a little bit longer. That I could be in this in-between space, where it's happening, but nothing bad has happened because of it.

If there's one thing I know all too well about life it's that time moves on relentlessly, even if you wanted to stop. You can't freeze moments. No matter how much you wish you could.

And so I have to accept that time is going to keep marching on, and this will finish, and it will be as bad an idea as seems, but at least I'll have had his hands on me.

I have to stop thinking. I have to just surrender.

I am – often – the enemy of my own pleasure. But this thing between the two of us is so powerful, I'm not sure that I'm strong enough to dampen the pleasure.

I'm the one who shifts, gets up on my knees so that I can pull my sweatpants down, work them down just enough, so that I can kick them off on the floor. I'm naked on his lap, and he's wearing just his underwear.

Now I feel like it's my turn.

I rock myself against him, as I press my hands against his chest. It's bare and gorgeous, and I cannot believe I'm touching Colt Campbell's chest. I'm naked, and I feel like touching his chest shouldn't necessarily be the thing making my circuits go haywire right now, but it feels like it is.

It really feels like it is.

I've never seen a more perfect man. Yes, now he has a scar on those gorgeous abs, but it doesn't make him any less hot.

I move my hands down his muscles, down to that scar, I trace it, just like I do every other line on his body. I let my fingertips brush his nipple, and he shivers beneath my hand.

"Fuck," he whispers.

I'm satisfied by that. I love that I'm making him tremble. That I'm making him swear. That I'm doing this to him. I love that he wants me.

I've never felt so beautiful. I never realized how much that would affect my own desire.

But then, I've also never been with a man that I found quite so gorgeous.

Because I never found another man this beautiful. Not ever.

It's him. It's always been him.

I know without a doubt that I'll have no trouble calling up the memory of his naked body. I know without a doubt that it will haunt me for the rest of my life, and it's a ghost that I'm choosing. It's a haunting that I would invite, a ritual summoning I would engage in every day no matter the consequences.

Yeah. He's worth it.

I nearly lost him.

My hands start shaking as I touch him. As I move to

touch his face again. I nearly lost him and we never experienced this. I nearly lost him and I never kissed him. I never felt him inside my body. I nearly lost him.

I grip his face and I kiss him, fiercely. Then, I'm all out of patience. I'm ready to reach into his underwear and grab his hard length, drag it out, and ride him, but he grips my chin, pulling me away, studying my gaze. "We need a condom."

"Oh," I whisper.

"My room."

I nod. I get up off of him, and I'm standing there naked in the middle of the living room at seven thirty in the morning. He looks at me, the broad light of day making the room bright. We have the blinds closed; no one can see in, but there's still a lot of natural light filtering in. I'm not embarrassed. Why would I be? He's looking at me like my body is something spectacular. He's looking at me like I'm amazing. I've never experienced anything like that before.

It makes me feel so alive. It makes me feel like a goddess. When I turn away from him, he makes a low sound in the back of his throat, and I smile just slightly and shake my ass just a little bit extra as I walk toward the bedroom.

I let out a long, shaking breath as soon as I get into the room. I put my hand on my chest and feel my heart raging. Then I steel myself and move over to the nightstand. There's a box of condoms in there. I take one out, and then I take another. Just in case. I go back into the living room, and he's waiting. My internal muscles clench as I stare at him. He's got his thighs spread wide, his injured leg out straight in front of him. I can see the hard, thick length of his erection about to burst through his underwear. The outline of him is compelling. I want to see more. But then there's everything else about him. His thick thighs, his impressive chest.

His face.

Oh, that face.

And all the ways that it's ever haunted me.

He smiles, and it's like something breaks open inside me. There's the charmer. This must be what other women see. What they have seen for years. I've never seen it. I've never seen him turned on. Never seen him in this mode. Charming. Seductive.

I don't even need him to do a thing. It's good all on its own. But I kind of like the thing. I feel like I've been led into a secret club. Not the most exclusive club, but one I've never been invited to before.

I grab hold of the condom and move toward the couch. But as I got to straddle his lap, he grabs my hip, pulls me up as he lies down on the couch, bringing me square over his face. I'm... I'm right against his mouth. He looks up at me, blue eyes wicked, and I almost passed out from just how outrageously dirty this is. How incredible it is.

I've never... I've never actually been on top of a man while this happened.

His two large hands go to grab my ass, and he pulls me firmly against his mouth as he begins to eat me. He licks me with long, sure strokes, sucking my clit into his mouth and making me cry out with pleasure.

"God," I whimper, grabbing hold of the back of the couch.

He lifts his head. "Just me. But I can see how you get the two confused."

And then, he's right back there. Licking me, sucking me, teasing me. He brings his thumbs up, spreading my lower lips, massaging either side of my clit while he continues to lick me. He pushes me so high, so fast, I barely recognize that I'm on the edge until I'm pushed over. I slam my hand down on the couch cushion, curling my fist around the fabric as I scream. I've never in all my life screamed during sex.

But I can't even believe this. This is the hottest...

I'm whimpering. Rolling my hips forward. I'm not embarrassed anymore. Not worried about anything. I'm just riding his face, taking every last gasp of pleasure that I can as he continues to lick, suck, tease.

His large hands are digging hard into my butt, his mouth working me over time. And it doesn't take long for a second orgasm to build. For me to break.

For me to lose it entirely.

I'm boneless when he finally sits up, and I would marvel at his strength, but I'm too busy marveling at everything else. "Condom," he says, his voice rough.

I scramble and reach out to the cushions, grab hold of the packet. Hand it to him. He tears it open, freeing himself from the black boxers, and rolling the condom over himself before I get a good look.

Even with it on, I can see how big he is. How... Yeah. I was right. I will remember his penis for the rest of my life.

In great detail.

It is the Holy Grail of dick.

The most gorgeous cock on any man, and I don't even need to see any more of them to know that.

Perfect for me.

I just know it.

"Ride me," he says, his voice rough.

I lift up my hips, my thighs shaking as I bring myself down onto him. Then he grabs the back of my head and brings me in for a fierce kiss. His tongue goes deep, and I can taste my own pleasure on him as I take him into my body, inch by excruciating inch.

I'm whimpering, trembling as he fills me. As Colt Campbell puts himself entirely inside me. Joins his body to mine.

I grip his shoulders, my nails digging in deep as I lift my hips and start to ride him. It's so good. So good. So perfect.

I can't breathe. I can't think.

All I can do is feel. The delicious friction of him inside of me. My breasts brushing against his chest with every stroke. I set the tempo. The rhythm. I'm sure he would rather be in charge. But I like that I've taken that from him. I can feel another orgasm building. That feels impossible. *Three?*

Not that I'm complaining.

He leans back, watching me, watching me move up and down on him, watching me take my pleasure.

And I love that I'm putting on a show for him. I've never been particularly repressed, I don't think, but I also can't remember ever relishing having a man look at me. Watching me pleasure myself. Maybe because I've never exactly pleasured myself on any of my other partners. Not like this.

He presses his thumb between my legs, rubbing it over my clit, and I lurch forward, nails digging into his shoulders as he wrenches another orgasm from me faster, harder than I expected.

"You're such a good girl," he says. "You act like a brat. We're just waiting for a man to make you sweet."

That shouldn't be hot. It shouldn't turn me on. It should make me mad. But instead, I feel myself close to the edge again. So close. So close.

Then he thrusts his hips up off the couch. Hard. Changes the rhythm, changes the game. I didn't realize how strong he was in this position, injured, how much force he could put behind it. But he's doing it. Hips working like a piston, driving deep. Hard.

I can see him going closer to the edge, his jaw locking together, the tendons in his neck standing out. He wraps one arm around my waist, his hand pressed against my shoulder blades as he thrusts into me one last time, roaring as he comes, as he pulses inside of me, drawing another shattering orgasm for me.

Four.

And that's when I melt against him. I melt like a candle held to a flame. Pliant wax that can't reform.

I'm still too hot. Still too rocked.

"What the hell have you done to me?"

"I was going to ask you the same question." He strokes my cheek, and I'm struck by the tenderness on his face. It creates a strange kind of fear response inside of me. I want to run away from it. Because I feel like I'm not looking at *him*, at least, not the version of him I know. I feel like... It's like something straight out of a dream that I would've had when I was too young to actually imagine sex.

When I thought only about the *feelings*, not the intense physicality.

Seeing this expression on his face feels illegal.

I have to turn away.

He taps my hip and I climb off of him. "Are you okay?" I ask, feeling worried I did something to hurt him.

He throws his head back, and he laughs. "Am I okay?" He laughs, and keeps on laughing. "That is the weirdest question I've ever been asked after sex."

"Well, I might have... Hurt you."

"I'm not hurt."

His gaze is roaming everywhere but my face. He seems

completely distracted from my body. And that I like. That doesn't freak me out. That makes me feel good, in fact.

"Do you need help with..." I look down meaningfully at his naked body. The condom.

"Please," he says. "I've got it. Just hand me my crutches."

I do, and I watch how much easier he's maneuvering now. Apparently, I didn't harm him with the vigorous sex.

Sex. Colt and I had sex. Oh God.

I sit down on the couch while he goes into the bathroom. I cover my mouth. I'm not sure whether to laugh or cry.

Chapter Eleven

Colt

I'm still not sure if I just had a fever dream or if all that really happened. Not even as I pull the condom off and throw it into the trash can do I really feel certain that it's reality.

Except my brain is buzzing, and my body feels more satisfied than it has in a hell of a long time, so it has to be real.

Yeah. It has to be real.

I just fucked my stepsister.

I look up, and I see my reflection in the mirror. I half expect to see a monster staring back at me. Because who does that? Who puts his entire family dynamic in jeopardy to get laid? I brace my hands on the counter.

"You do," I say to my reflection. "You do. You're your fucking dad."

Ouch. That actually hurts. Even though it came from me.

I feel gross. That comparison makes me feel gross. The sex with Allison made me feel great. It's more that I *wish* I could regret it. That's the problem. I know that I should. I know the comparison to my dad is apt. Because he was definitely the kind of man who took his pleasure into consideration far above what anyone in the situation needed.

I let her smooth-talk the consequences away. I didn't have to do that. I knew exactly what I was doing. And part of me relished it.

Because my attraction to her has been the one taboo thing that I've avoided all this time. My attraction to her has been something that I've suppressed.

So when she came in, looking so cute in that sweatsuit, wearing nothing underneath it – I just had a feeling, given that she was obviously right out of the shower – I thought... Why not? Why shouldn't I have her? I'm being denied the rodeo. I'm being denied my physical fitness. My good health. Denying myself Allison feels like one thing too many. Once she kissed me... It was over.

"Scumbag," I say to my reflection. I wait to be bothered by it.

I'm just not.

I take a deep breath and pause in my bedroom. I decide that I need to get dressed before going out there. Walking on crutches naked is kind of absurd. I don't need any visible bouncing happening in front of her.

I scowl as I dress. I'm not entirely steady after what just happened.

I come out into the living room, and she's also dressed. Her hair is still wet, and she's sitting there on the couch cross-legged, looking small and vulnerable, and making me feel just awful.

"Are you okay?"

"Oh, I'm good," she says. She looks up at me, her expression dreamy. "I'm literally just zoning out because I'm having an orgasm high."

My ego jumps up inside me and requests a high five. I don't honor that. But it feels good. It really does feel good. And I feel like maybe I'm not entirely broken.

So. That's exactly what she wanted. For me to feel better about myself. She wanted to know that sex can be great. I provided it.

"Did I exceed expectations?"

"Yes," she says. She tucks a strand of hair behind her ear. "That was amazing."

Silence stretches between us. We never had the closest relationship. I don't always know what to say to her. We're better when we're sniping at each other than when we're trying to make serious conversation. Whenever we try, it usually ends badly. Sincerity would be great right now. It would be the right thing. But I don't especially know how to wield it.

"I'm probably going to move," she says.

"What?"

"When my rotations start? I think I am going to move. I think I'll even look for an apartment. Something small, something I don't have to really keep up. Because I'm going to have so much work to do."

"Okay." I'm not sure where this is going.

"It'll be about a week into the new term. After the break. I have a feeling you'll be in a way better position and..."

"Are you... About to suggest that we keep doing this until you leave?"

She looks away from me, and not slowly. "Yes. I am about to suggest that. Because I think... I don't think it's reasonable to expect the two of us are going to be around each other and not want to do this. You're stuck in the house..."

"Are you suggesting sex as a boredom buster?"

"Kind of," she says. "But is it a bad suggestion?"

"No," I say. I'm definitely not bored. I don't feel hopeless. I don't have images of my near-death dancing in my head, so I guess sex is the therapy that I've been waiting for all this time, even if I didn't really know it.

"So you just want to keep doing this."

"Yes. I do. Because we already did. And you can't put the horse back in the barn once it's bolted."

"I've heard that."

"We already have to keep it a secret."

"Yeah. Definitely."

"So it just seems reasonable that we might keep going with it. Because we've already earned whatever the consequences are."

I don't even want to argue with that. That, I think, is probably sex logic. But I don't really care. I also don't really know what to do. I've never been in a relationship; that's not what this is. But she's somebody that I know better than the average bed partner, and I feel like I should sit with her. Touch her. But also, I'm not sure romance feels exactly like the right thing. Especially given the fact that we've both firmly established this is just physical, and things are going to go back to normal when we put an end to it. Actually, I think she's smart. My healing, her moving, it'll be an easy line to draw under it. And that's the thing. We need clear lines, clear boundaries. An endpoint.

We have the endpoint.

"Do you want me to hold you?"

She lifts her head. "I... Yes."

There. That's what she wants. I maneuver myself down on the couch next to her, and I pull her into my arms. She takes a deep breath and rests her head on my chest. We sit for a moment like that. And I don't question the contentedness coursing through my veins. It was good sex.

Great sex.

It fixed something inside of me. I'm sure of that much, even if I'm not sure of anything else.

So I sit with her like that, and I honestly can't remember the last time my soul felt that quiet. Because there's always something. The next ride, the next high.

But for some reason right now, I'm not worried about the future. I'm just feeling. We don't have the TV on. She's just resting her head against my chest. I look at her hair. That beautiful, red hair. Drying now, post-shower. It's a little curlier than usual.

I push my fingers through the silky strands.

She's beautiful. And I can finally let myself feel that. Know it. Fully engage with it. I can finally feel it.

"What are your plans today?" I ask.

She huffs. "I don't have any. I mean, I don't work today, and the term ended so...

"Well, I don't have any plans. Because I'm a shut-in now."

"Do you want to try to not be a shut-in?"

"I..." I think about going out in town. With my body the way that it is. All my injuries.

"What if we drove to a different town?" she says. Like she can read my mind.

"Oh. Yeah. I would be interested in that."

The pressure of being me, in this town... that sounds so egotistical. I don't like it. But it's true. There are expectations of me. And anything short of a faith healing in public feels like I'm letting people down.

I know that's not true. I know it's not fair. But it is what it feels like.

"We can go to the grocery store, grab some lunch."

"Yeah. I... I'd like that. Especially since I went to all the trouble to get dressed up."

"So dressed up," she says, poking me in the ribs.

There is such a casual intimacy to the touch. Before this, there hasn't been any casual intimacy between us. There's barely been casual friendliness.

There's no real tension in our family. Except between us. We're the tension. We're the problem. We're the two who have the power to break everything apart.

The power to take something great and easy and beautiful and turn it into something fraught and awful.

So we have to not do that.

But the truth is, whether we'd actually had sex or not, things had shifted between us, and the change was made.

She's right about that.

Right about bolting horses, and how you can't put them back into the barn.

My hand is on her hip. Just like the other day when she almost fell. I look at it. She's not moving away from me now.

"When do you want to go?"

"Well," I say slowly, my eye still trained on where my hand meets her hip. "I'd like to have some coffee. Get my head on straight. And then we can drive over to Tolowa. Do a little grocery shopping. Get some hamburgers."

She squints at me. "I didn't agree to hamburgers."

"But I want one."

"You can get that here. We should get Thai food. Because we can't get that here."

"I don't want that. And I'm injured."

"You're starting to push it," she says.

"Hey. How is asking to be babied pushing it? I was told yesterday, quite forcefully, that I need to lean into my infirmity."

"I don't think I ever said that."

She gets up and walks into the kitchen. I watch her for a moment, my eyes trained on her backside. Now I know what it looks like completely naked. I look up at the ceiling and try to keep myself from getting another erection. How funny. I didn't have a single one for ages. And now here we are.

I stand up slowly, and make my way in after her.

"I'm going to have to go home and get dressed at some point," she says.

"Really? I like this."

"That's nice," she says. "But I don't think it's appropriate for grocery shopping."

"Not true. Plenty of people wear their pajamas grocery shopping. Hell, the toughest girls you know wear their cookie monster pajamas out to the grocery store."

She frowns. "True. But those girls always have your back."

"It's true. Unlike the girl in the Tweety Bird pajamas. They're just mean for no reason."

She laughs. And I have this strange sense that I've missed an awful lot not having a real relationship with her over these last few years. We could have had this. Could've talked and joked. Sex aside, things have been difficult between us. They always have.

I *do* like her.

All this time I've cast her as the younger sister figure, it was convenient for me to do it.

It made sure that nothing got messy. And it was always ripe for messiness. No matter how much I might pretend otherwise. Because I noticed when she became a woman. I noticed that she was beautiful. In a way that I knew wasn't right for me to be noticing my stepsister. I didn't live at home anymore, she was over eighteen, it's not like there was anything... Nothing dodgy about it in that way. But definitely not right.

Too late to be thinking about all that now, I suppose. It's weird, though, how this doesn't feel wrong. It feels good. My body feels good for the first time in a hell of a long while.

I watch her make the coffee, because I'm enjoying watching her movements in a different way. Taking in what she does, the way that her hair catches the sunlight, how it falls over her shoulders. The way her elegant fingers maneuver around all the things in the kitchen. The way her hips sway when she walks. I've seen all these things before, but this is the first time I've ever let myself notice them in this way.

This time when we sit together at the table it doesn't feel fraught. It feels easy. Though, there is a threat of underlying tension between us, but now I know what it is. Sexual tension. Has it been that way for a long time? Is that what drives the tense moments between us? Entirely possible.

And now we can just have sex instead of fighting.

I love that for us.

She finishes her cup of coffee, and sets it down at the center of the table. "I'm going to go get dressed. I'll be back in like fifteen minutes, and then we can go."

I don't want her to leave. I can't say that I've ever had that experience before after sex with a woman. Usually I'm amped for some alone time. Not now. A combination of the fact that I'm not enjoying being alone with my demons right now, and her, I suspect.

The minutes go by slowly, and when she comes back again I practically leap toward the front door.

I feel like a dog that's been in his kennel for too long. Yeah, we went to my parents' house, but that's not the same.

"Your mom must've told everyone to stay away," she muses as we get into my truck.

"You think?"

"Oh yeah," she says, starting the ignition. "Otherwise you'd be inundated with women holding casseroles offering to hand out condolence blow jobs."

I nearly choked on my own breath as we pull out on the street. "Excuse me?"

"Oh, come on. You know it's true."

"I don't know that it's true."

"Everyone's going to want to be part of your healing, Colt."

There is a slight crispness to her tone, and I wonder what she did to make yourself mad at me when she went over to change.

"What have you been thinking about?"

"Nothing."

"You have been. You've been thinking about me getting Get Well Soon Blow Jobs, which, as it happens, is kind of an upgrade from a mylar balloon. But a strange route to take."

She gives me a deadly glare from the corner of her eye.

"I don't want anyone else," I say.

She turns toward me quickly, then turns back so that she's facing the road. "You think that because... You feel insecure."

"I feel *insecure*. I *feel* insecure. *I* feel insecure? I put an emphasis on a different word every time I repeated. "First of all, you've seen my dick."

She surprises me by bursting out laughing. "Yes. I have."

"So I'm not entirely sure where you think my insecurity is supposed to come from."

"You're just... You're injured."

"How many times did you come?"

"Colt," she says. "I'm serious."

"Listen, this is what we aren't going to do, Allison, we are not going to minimize this. Okay? Yes, we have to keep it a secret, yes, it's for a limited time. We both know that's the only way that it can happen, we both know that's the only thing. The only way that it can be. But I... Hell, I thought you were beautiful for years."

"You have not," she says.

"I have. I fucking have. I just suppressed it. And you know, when I move all the time, it's easy for me to pretend that there's nothing there. I don't feel anything. It's easy for me to pretend that we haven't got a thing between us, okay? But the reality is, we do. And we've proven that. Solidly. This morning was... It was amazing. It was better for me, too. Different for me. Okay?"

I feel raw from admission, but it is true. And hell yeah, the circumstances might be part of it, but they aren't the whole thing.

"Why didn't you tell me that you wanted me before?"

"Why didn't I tell you before this morning, or why didn't I tell you this morning?"

"Well. This morning. Or yesterday, when you almost kissed me out in the backyard. It hurt my feelings and... You could've just said this then."

"I could have. But I was still trying to figure it all out.

And by the time I stormed into the house last night, I wasn't thinking about anything. I wasn't trying to figure anything out anymore, I was just having a fit because I felt shitty, and I didn't know what else to do. But yeah, I have felt attraction to you before. You make it easy to steer clear of you, though, because you steer clear of me."

"Because I'm attracted to you," she says, sounding just as frustrated as I do. "I don't want it, I didn't ask for it, but I just... I am. I have been. It sucks, and I hate it. Thanks."

"You're welcome?" I shake my head. "I just don't want you to run with this idea that I could just as easily take a casserole and an orgasm from Jenny down the block, okay?"

"Who's Jenny?"

"She's hypothetical. Okay? The point is, I haven't felt desire for anyone else. I haven't even felt like getting myself off, okay? You said that I was going to seduce a nurse in the hospital, but I didn't even have an inkling toward that. It's you. It's not sex or just the amount of time that it's been, it's you. My proximity to you. I don't know how to explain it, I don't know how to make it okay, I don't know what to do with it exactly. But that's where we are. And I don't want to hurt you. But I really, really don't want you to think you're interchangeable. You're not." It's the most heartfelt speech I've ever made to a woman.

But I need her to know that. Because yeah, part of this is that I'm feeling more like myself. Part of it is that this wouldn't have happened if not for the accident, but it's complicated. It has to do with proximity, me slowing down, it has to do with all this stuff that isn't her being second best, or whatever she thinks this is.

"I believe you," she says.

That means more to me than I can articulate. I didn't realize I needed her to believe me. That I needed to feel like

I wasn't just my dad. Like I'm not just using her for my own pleasure.

"It's just you and me for the next bit, okay?"

"Okay," she says.

She looks at me just quickly again, and I see a slight smile on her face.

I'm rarely the reason Allison smiles. So I'll take it.

"Do you have any favorite foods that you want to get?"

I actually eat pretty clean when I am in season on the rodeo. It would be nice to just drink a lot of beer and barbecue, but I take really good care of myself. Which is kind of hilarious now.

"Is it weird that I want vegetables. And also cake?"

"No," she says. "Nothing is weird. I mean, because everything is weird, to be clear."

"That's the truth."

Yeah. Everything was weird. So it's best to just take a free fall into it, I guess.

When we arrive in Tolowa, she chooses one of the biggest grocery stores there. It has a lot of specialty foods, a lot of healthy, organic things, but also a big bakery, and some international goodies. It's overpriced, and I'm thrilled, because I plan on indulging myself.

"I'll make a salad tonight," I say.

She wrinkles her nose. "You'll make it?"

"Yeah. It's getting easier for me to walk on the crutches. Nothing hurts quite as bad as it did a week ago. Let alone three weeks ago. I think I'll be totally fine making part of dinner."

"Well, I'll take it."

We end up deciding on some fresh pasta and lots of vegetables along with an Alfredo sauce. There's great sourdough bread in the bakery, and also a cake that looks like it came straight from heaven. I want a little bit of normalcy, and a little bit of indulgence. That seems about right to me.

She's pushing the cart, which I don't love, but there really wouldn't be an easy way for me to manage crutches and the cart. I could probably figure it out if I absolutely had to, but it's easier to let her take the wheel. By the end, we got a little bit overkill, snacks, sweets, dressings, sauces, overfilling the cart. But there's something easy about spending this time with her. Something cheerful about it. Maybe it's just being up and out of the house. Somewhere other than my parents' house. Maybe that's what it is.

Or maybe it's being with her.

She has insulated bags in the back of the car, with ice packs, and we fill those up before heading to lunch.

"Anywhere else you want to stop?"

"No."

"You don't want to get some new Wranglers cut up?"

"I'd like to not need any more than I have. Unless I do end up having to start that exhibitionist only fans."

"Are you really worried about that?"

"Do I think I'm really going to have to start an OnlyFans?"

"No. I mean, are you really worried that you're not going to be able to go back to the rodeo?"

I finish putting the last bag into the trunk. Then I get into the passenger seat. Her question is rattling around uncomfortably inside me, and I don't know how to answer it. She gets in the car, moments after I do, starting the ignition. "Sorry. I guess you probably can't answer that right now."

"No. I can. Yeah. I'm worried about not being able to go back to the rodeo. But I guess I'm worried about it... It's not just the physical. It's the mental stuff."

"You didn't even want the bull to be put down right after it happened."

"I still don't. But I also wonder if it's a sign that I don't need to be doing this anymore. It also feels like unfinished business, and I hate that. I want to go back. I want to be able to finish. I want to be able to win. But I don't know if I'm going to be able to do that. I don't know how things are going to change. When I'm by myself, I just relive parts of the accident. Over and over again." Suddenly, I feel like I've been slugged in the gut. "I almost died, Allison."

She reaches across the expanse of the car and puts her hand on my knee. "I know. Watching that happen to you was the single worst thing that I've ever experienced."

She watched her mom die. Slowly. It was a tragedy. And she's saying my accident was the worst thing she's ever seen?

"It was so violent," she says. And there was nothing we could do. We were just so helpless. It was so fast and brutal. Disease is a terrible thing. It can move fast, and it can move slow. In my mom's case, it took years. Years for it to finally be finished with her. Years for it to all be over. That's been my experience with loss. But that... It was so violent. So sudden. I've seen you ride I don't know how many times. Nothing like that. Ever."

"I know. I mean, obviously I never expected that. You know that it's possible. They're animals. In the minute you bring animals into anything you've brought in a variable that you can't control. You can't predict it. You can anticipate it. Probability goes right out the fucking window. The odds are in your favor, I suppose. But the reality is, the next bull could have done the same thing to his rider, and the next, odds be damned. Because animals are random. Just because it doesn't often happen, doesn't mean it couldn't. I was cocky. I was egotistical. And I thought that I was bulletproof. But now I don't think that I am." I pause, trying to gather my thoughts, my emotions. "I don't know how to stand in front of the firing squad knowing that I can be killed."

We just sit there like that for a moment.

"If you don't want to go back, you don't have to."

"I know. But I'm scared of being somebody that I don't recognize. I'm afraid of losing my edge. I'm afraid of... It's the one place that I put all of my intensity. My ambition. Because I always had to be easy. I always had to make things easy for my mom. I just wanted to... Delight her, I guess. Make her happy. I wanted to give her the kid she deserved to have. For sticking with me. For being there for me when my dad wasn't."

"You're allowed to be unhappy. You're allowed to have problems. You're allowed to be difficult."

"I'm not, though," I say, the words torn from me. "I'm not."

I take a deep breath. "You were really the only person I could ever be... You're the only person that I tease, really. You're the only person who sees that part of me. Because you're the only one that I feel safe with."

Those words sit strangely on my tongue. I feel like I've admitted some kind of weakness. This deep fear that I have of being too difficult, of being abandoned. This need. It's not just about my mom, it's about me. I want everybody to look and see how special I am. Because if they see how special I am then I'm somebody who didn't deserve to be abandoned. And that means putting on a show.

A performance.

I'm not the Golden Boy of Gold Valley by accident.

I am very much that on purpose, and it's hard-won. And

I don't feel like I have it in me anymore. I don't feel like I have it in me right now. I'm not sure that I ever will again. That's why we had to come out here to go grocery shopping so that I didn't feel like I was going to crush someone beneath the weight of their own disappointment for how I'm just normal.

"I'm a narcissist," I say.

"No, you aren't," she says, finally pulling the car out of his parking space and heading out of the parking lot.

"I think so much about putting on performances for other people, but all that is is... Making myself really important to the story."

"We're all the main characters in our own story."

"Yeah. But it's not like there's a spotlight on me all the time."

"There actually is, Colt," she says. "I don't know if that really helps you right now. That visual. But I've always felt like you had a spotlight on you. Like you were the sort of magical being that everybody wanted to be around. You were always half of the conversations in the halls at school. And you weren't even at my school half the time. People were obsessed with getting information about you. Girls would harass me all the time. In fact, I had to worry about girls becoming friends with me so that they could have sleepovers at my house, just so they could have sleepovers at your house. You're one-of-a-kind. You are special."

"But everyone is."

She looks over at me. "Not in the same way."

"That's not true. I'm not... I'm just performing. That's what everyone likes. Always a joke. Always a smile. Always a new win. Captain of the football team, whatever. It's just a tap dance routine. And when the tap dance routine is over who's going to stay?"

"Me."

I look over at her, our eyes meet for a moment before she turns her focus back to the road.

"Thanks."

"No problem."

She takes me to a restaurant with hamburgers – no argument – and I order a cheeseburger while she goes with salad.

"I'm making you a salad tonight," I say.

"I know. But we are also making pasta with cream sauce. So, I'm going to pace myself. Also, we have that cake." The cake at least, is a pretty cheery addition to things.

We head out of the restaurant, and I breathe in the warm air. It's beautiful, this place. It's not going to be too hard being home more. Being in Oregon. I do love it here.

"You okay?" She bumps up beside me, and her palm presses to mine, and before I can think about it, I'm lacing my fingers through hers, and we are holding hands.

Neither of us speaks, and we walk to the car together like that. I open her door for her, managing to do all that while still walking on crutches. It is possible. I feel better. More in control of my body. As the wound in my midsection heals, my ability to maneuver gets easier. I don't need to rely on my still-injured leg quite as much. I don't default to putting weight on that side of my body. But mainly, I just like feeling functional. For her. With her. I like not feeling like I need everything done for me.

I know what she said is true. That I would feel differently if it were somebody else. That I wouldn't think that they only had value if their body went back to the way it had always been. Of course I wouldn't think that. But I just feel differently about myself. And I hate the idea that I might have to change my thinking. I don't want to change. I get into the car, and buckle myself in.

"I might have to change." It's not even a fully formed thought, and I said it out loud to her.

"Your clothes? Or philosophically."

"Philosophically. I don't want to."

"I don't know that anybody wants to."

"Yeah. It's just hard."

"I know. I mean, I don't know, because it's not something that really happened to me. But my mom – I hate to keep comparing you, it's just I see parallels. After she did treatment the first time, she always got tired a little bit easier. It just changed things for her. And there were always new medications and new treatments, and they had responses in her body. Some affected her terribly, and some made it so she could pretty much go about her daily life. It all just depended on where she was in the remission cycle. But I loved her just the same. No matter what. We all did. And sometimes we had to change what we did. What we didn't do. But it didn't change how we felt about her."

"I get that. I do." Except all my relationships feel more tentative than that, and I have a feeling that's on me. I have a feeling that's about my own stuff. My own baggage. What I feel and don't feel in those relationships.

"I'm just saying. Having to face down change is kind of a terrible thing. But eventually, you're just living it. And everything will fall into place."

I hope that's true. I really do.

I take a nap when we get home, because it's actually been kind of a long, weird day. And when I get up, she's in the kitchen putting a pot of pasta on the stovetop.

"I'll get to making that salad."

I fetch a cutting board, and a knife. I find a good way to

brace myself against the counter, and start chopping vegetables methodically.

"I really don't want you to lose your balance while you're holding that knife."

"It's fine," I say. "If there's one thing I'm pretty confident with... Well, it's sex. But if there's another thing, it's that I do know my way around the kitchen."

"I guess you do." Her forehead creases. "That's kind of a weird skill for you to have."

I notice she ignores my comment about sex. "Not really. I used to cook when I was a kid."

"You did?"

"Oh, when my mom was getting her real estate business up and running she would have really long days. I got good at cooking. I got good at... Making things easier for her."

I hear my own childhood trauma coming out of my mouth again. But is it really trauma if you had a wonderful parent? Is it really trauma if it taught you life skills that are very valuable? Everyone should know how to cook for themselves. I'm an athlete, so knowing how to make healthy meals has been an asset. So yeah. It's not like it's wasted effort. It's not like it's something that did me long-term harm.

"I'm good," I say.

"You seem like it." I don't think she means that.

"I like cooking for her. I still do."

"Well, I appreciate you cooking for me."

She's clearly decided to let me off the hook with this one. I add rosemary croissant croutons, some chevre, Craisins, a cucumber, and artichoke hearts to the salad. I toss it in balsamic vinaigrette, and by the time I'm done with that, the noodles are through cooking, and her vegetable sauce is done marrying ingredients. "Let's eat on the patio."

I'm usually a beer guy, but this seems like a good time for wine, which she seems content with.

"Remember when we took you out to the Gold Valley Saloon for your birthday?" I ask.

She gives me a pointed glare. "Yes."

"You drank so many daiquiris."

"Yes. Well. It was my birthday. That's what you're there for."

"Gentry practically had to cart you out of there in a wheelbarrow."

"It was fun."

"Yeah. It was. Then you were beautiful. I couldn't stop staring at you." The memory makes my stomach tighten. It's one of those things that I've been pushing away ever since. But she was just so cute and giggly that night. Happy. Dancing with Lily, attracting attention from everywhere. She's lovely. She had a boyfriend at the time, and he was there, enjoying things, and probably thinking he was going to get lucky. He probably did.

She's never had difficulty attracting a man. But apparently, none of them have done right by her. So I reserve the right to be annoyed at them. A woman as pretty as her deserves more than men who are just using her to have their own pleasure. A man has to appreciate a woman's body if he's going to have it shared with him, in my opinion. Has to be just as invested in her pleasure as he is in his own. Hell, *more* so. That's just what I think.

"I was beautiful?" she asks.

"Yeah." I reach out and take a strand of her hair between my fingers. "It made me mad."

"Why?"

"I guess for the same reason I make you mad."

She ducks her head. "No comment."

"You were dating... What's his name?"

She rolls her eyes. "Yeah. I was."

"And he was bad in bed."

"We've established this."

"Interesting."

"Well, if you had offered that night, I would've gone home with you."

My stomach goes tight, pleasure brushing down to my groin. I want her again. And we've already done away with all the explanations, potential recriminations, and what-ifs. We're just doing this.

I wait impatiently for her to finish her meal. Her glass of wine.

Then I lean in, cup her face, and watch as her pupils expand, as her breath catches. I feel an answering response in my own body. My own need building. I kiss her then. It's even sweeter than I remember. Even better than it was this morning. When she kissed me up against the wall I was shocked. Now I'm in control. Licking her lower lip, her upper lip, nipping her, sucking that lip into my mouth. She groans, her hand going to my thigh underneath the table, nails digging into me.

"I should've had you then," I whisper against her mouth. "But I didn't. I have you now, though."

"Please," she whispers.

I want to pick her up and carry her to bed. I want to throw her around and give her a good athletic fuck. I want to take her in the shower, against the wall, and I can't do any of that. At the moment, I don't actually care if I ever ride again. What I want is to be able to take her, anyway I want.

She'll be gone by then. And you won't be doing this anymore. I don't like that realization, so I push it to the side. There's quite enough happening in my life right now that I don't want to face. I don't need to be bracing really realistic about this.

"Come to bed," I say.

She nods slowly, and stands up, then she's the one who reaches her hand out, and I take it. We walk together to the bedroom, and I wrap my arms around her, kissing her hard and deep. And I decide that I'm good to have her just like I want her. I will figure it out.

But while I'm thinking of that, she's pawing at my shirt.

I strip it up over my head, and she leans in, licking my chest, moving her hands down my midsection, down my stomach. Letting her tongue blaze a trail down to the waistband of my ruined jeans.

She undoes my belt. I sit down on the bed, because I know I'm not going to be able to keep steady if she's headed for what I think she is.

"I know I didn't make a casserole tonight, but am I allowed to give you a blow job?"

Need courses through me, a fierce, possessive yes echoing inside of me. I growl, my hand going to her hair, forcing her face up to meet my gaze. "Yes, you have my permission." I'm supposed to be teasing, but it doesn't come out light. Doesn't come across as a joke. Instead, my voice sounds tortured. Dominant in a way that I'm usually not in the bedroom.

I like to take charge in small ways. I like to be the strong one. But I don't need to play power exchange games. For the first time, I kind of get the appeal. She undoes the snap on my jeans, the zipper, frees my cock and leans in, her tongue darting out to the head, pleasure cascading over me at a wave.

She presses her soft lips to me.

A kiss.

A kiss of all things. And I'm dying. Then, she sucks me in deep, swallowing me down. She makes eye contact with me, those beautiful green eyes on mine as she tastes me. I start to arch my hips up off the mattress, unable to control myself. Unable to hold back. I'm still holding her hair, thrusting up against the back of her throat.

She's taking me like a champ.

And I do pull her hair now. I'm rewarded with a rough sound of pleasure from her that echoes through me.

It's the best fucking blow job I've ever had in my life. She is in possession of this level of skill, and those assholes she's been sleeping with can't be bothered to make her come? Pearls before swine. Pearls before God damn pigs.

She deserves so much more. She's a queen. A goddess.

I thrust upward, and she brings her head down even more aggressively, a guttural sound in the back of her throat. I gasped, then pulled her away quickly, because I'm about to lose it. She wipes at her mouth, dainty, sweet. Hell, that wasn't either of those things.

"I could've kept going," she says.

"Why didn't you ever tell me you could do that?"

"It's not something that comes up in polite conversation. Though I have to say, I've never put myself to the test quite like that."

Oh my ego is out of control now. My hand still fisted in her hair I draw her up and bring her in for a kiss. My arm wrapped around her waist, I practically bring her up onto my lap. And then, I reverse our positions. I've got my leg and the brace off the bed, my toe barely making contact with the ground but not bearing any weight. My other leg is on the bed, my knee pressed into the mattress. "I want to fuck you," I say.

"I thought that was the idea."

"No. Like this."

I'm over her, my eyes blazing into hers.

"I don't want you to hurt yourself."

I growl. "I've got it."

With a look of desperation on her face, she reaches over to the nightstand and paws around for a condom. She reminds me of a video that I saw of a raccoon trying to grab dog food while not looking. But she resurfaces with the condom, and tears it open quickly. Then she reaches between us, and rolls it over me. Squeezes me for good measure.

I let my head fall back. God it feels good. She feels good.

This feels good. She brings out a whole lot of things in me that I've never explored. This desire for the forbidden. Enjoying more intensity during sex. Who would've ever thought that my stepsister was the key to unlocking all that.

I draw up her thigh and bring it up over my hip as I sink slowly into her tight heat. She feels so good. So tight. So perfect. I start to move, and she's so slick and wet, it's perfect. Easy. But I don't let it stay easy. I take her hard, and her fingernails dig into my shoulders. I hope that she draws blood. Damn it all if I have to be marked by life, then I want some scars from this.

I whisper in her ear, rough, crude commands that seem to only get her more excited. And then I can feel her coming around my cock, her pleasure so explosive, so intense, that I'm afraid it's going to send me over right then too. That my own orgasm is going to be so hard, so intense, that my remaining whole bones are going to burst into smithereens.

When it does come, I might as well be getting thrown down into the arena again. That's how intense it is. That's how raw. And I wouldn't change it. It's perfect. It's everything.

I rest my forehead against hers, breathing hard. We're both sweaty. "Shower," I say.

"But you..."

"I'll sit on my bench," I say. "With my sad leg condom."

Suddenly, the sexy shower doesn't seem all that sexy. I regret suggesting it, but she doesn't seem to mind. Instead, she helps me get ready. And then, while I sit on the bench and shower, she stands across from me, naked, perfectly dry, waiting her turn.

"It's impractical," I say. "But it's a damn good show."

"I don't really mind it either. When I walked in the other morning, I..."

"That's why you were so embarrassed. Because you actually do want to see me naked."

"Well, yeah. I thought that was pretty obvious."

"Not to me. Because I didn't figure... Well. You know."

"Right. It's impossible. No one would ever suspect this."

She smiles. And it's wicked. I want her to stay the night with me. I make that decision then and there. Tonight, she's mine. And I'm not going to take any arguments about that.

Chapter Twelve

Allison

When I wake up in the morning, I'm completely tangled around Colt. It doesn't take me even a second to remember where I am or who I'm with. My body is raw and wrung out. I think we had sex four times after we got out of the shower. It doesn't even seem possible. That's a total of six times in one day. Granted, there were about ten hours between the first two times, but the others... He's incredible. And every single time he gave me orgasms that just about sent me into space.

It's still dark outside, I'm not sure what time it is. I peer over his broad shoulder at the clock on the nightstand. Not quite six. Then I kiss him on the shoulder, and roll out of bed. I need some coffee. Yesterday was just so... nice. I'm not sure I really thought we could have anything that nice.

Even in my wildest sex dreams, I suppose I always thought that if he and I hooked up, it would still be that same snarky, snippy, thing we always have. But yesterday was something deeper. Of course, I don't know how you can do all those things to someone else's body and not feel closer to them. It's either that or not be able to look them in the eye.

And his eyes are too pretty for me to never be able to look at them again.

So, accepting that we're mutually sexually destructive and filthy is our only option, really.

I'm not sure if I like it. It would be more comfortable if we were just what we were. If sex didn't change anything. I've had plenty of non-transformative sex. Of course with him it would be different. I should have known.

Right now, though, it's just us. There is no one else involved in this. It's just us.

And maybe it doesn't matter that it's changing things, because we are in this little cocoon. I feel guilty thinking of his injury as protective in some ways. But it is. It gives us this buffer. This time.

He wakes up, rolls over to me, and pulls me into his arms. And wakes me up the same way he put me to sleep.

And that's how things are. For a couple of weeks. Just the two of us running on orgasms and lack of sleep. Sitting together on the couch, me wearing my hoodie and curled up in his lap. Him curled up in mine. I've watched more baseball than I ever care to see again. We find reasons not to go to our parents' house for dinner together. He goes once without me, and I go without him. Gentry and Lily drive him, though, the truth is he could probably drive himself at this point.

I've spent every night at his house, and I have some conflicting feelings about that. About whether or not I should be doing it. Whether or not we should be this careless. But we are.

We've burned through so many condoms that I had to get more. I absolutely did a grocery order just for that. I didn't want to go in person to get them, which is funny, because I wouldn't normally think that much about it. But knowing who I'm using them with... Yeah. That is the issue. At least, I'm worried that people will somehow magically see through my brain and get visions of who it is I'm sleeping with. Can't have that.

No. I can't have that.

This is fake, and I know it. But there's been some very real stuff in the middle of it all.

We've talked more than we ever have. Even though he's been my stepbrother for about ten years, he's never been my friend. He was always Gentry's friend. There was a very clear line between Colt and me. Now, that line really isn't there. I haven't told him everything. Like how intense my crush on him was, or why I went and lost my virginity when I was sixteen, to escape the gagging desire that I felt for him. I don't know that there's any reason to debase myself.

But we shared a lot of things. Him not having his dad, and me not having my mom affected us. Still affects us. And the way my dad, his mom, have healed parts of us by being the best stepparents imaginable.

He's a lot more mobile on his crutches than he was a month ago. It's not even comparable. It makes me wonder if he really will surprise everybody. If he really will heal better than anybody thought. If I were in a different place with him emotionally, I think that would annoy me. That somehow Colt Campbell was managing to dodge the serious repercussions of his injury. Of course, I could never really be annoyed about that. I don't want him hurt.

I also don't really want to leave again.

But he will. So will I. Fall term, I'll be out of here. He'll be doing well enough that he might even be off his crutches.

"I have the day off," I say that morning as I make coffee. "I was kind of wondering if you wanted to go to Medicine Lake?"

"Oh. Why Medicine Lake?"

"Because it's a long drive on a winding road and it's a Tuesday, so probably nobody will be there?"

In my opinion, it's one of the most beautiful lakes in the area, but it's not as popular as some of the larger lakes, you aren't allowed to have motor craft on it, and it's about ten miles of gravel, then a hike down to the water. But it's clear, pristine and lovely, and I would really like the chance to be alone with him again, but somewhere not in the house.

Because the truth is, he's getting well enough to start doing things in town, and he should. Because the truth is, we can't hide forever.

It's going to be strange when we have to include other people in our lives, but it's going to happen. Hell, it even needs to happen.

But until then, I just want to enjoy this.

"Yeah. That sounds good. I can't swim in the lake, though."

"I know. But we can just look at it."

"I am antsy to get out of the house."

"Do you think you might enjoy... I don't know, going to the saloon?"

The last time we talked about him going out and about in town on his crutches, he was pretty leery.

But this time, he nods slowly. "Yeah. I think I might like that. Maybe we can go out with Dallas and Sarah, that would be fun."

"Yeah."

Neither of us says that it sort of seems like a double date. But I wonder if he's thinking the same thing I am. Of course, nobody would ever think that, because we are... Well, as far as the town is concerned, we are related. As far as I'm concerned, we are definitely not. By marriage, I suppose, but not in the way that makes this more than taboo.

"We can invite Gentry and Lily," he says.

Oh right. So he did think the same thing.

"Yeah. Let's do that."

I decide to prepare a picnic for today's trek, and he goes to take a shower. It's so domestic. And it's funny that I would even think that, because he and I lived together back all that time ago and we weren't anything like domestic. And now little bits of everyday routine are part of us. It makes me happy, and in a way that I'm a little bit afraid to admit. Makes me happy in a way that makes me uncomfortable, honestly.

That's a problem for the future. It's definitely not something that we need to worry about now. I don't think about any of those problems. Not while we drive out to the lake. It's a beautiful day. We go in his truck because that's the best for gravel, and I'm pleased when we don't see another car on the road leading up to the water. We're rewarded by there being no one there.

This is just so perfect. Idyllic.

Romantic. There is building friendship between us, there's sex, but romance...

I don't really know where that line begins to blur, I guess. We sit together, he holds on to me on the couch. He holds my hand.

As I look around the beautiful spot, the surface of the

lake glistening in the sunshine like diamonds, the tall green pines swaying gently, the velvet grass dotted with pink flowers. Birds chirping.

Oh God. This is *romantic*.

As we walk together to the plush grass just above the lake shore, I find myself completely frozen by that realization. That I'm taking him on a date. It's that I'm advancing this beyond sex and companionship to something more. Or maybe I'm not. Maybe this is a normal sort of thing. Maybe.

Maybe this is just part of me helping him heal. Yeah. I do have a strong instinct toward that. It's my vocation, after all.

I look at him, at his profile, his strong jaw. I have a sudden realization that I really wish I weren't having. He's healing something in me. Because there's some kind of profound joy in this. A real sort of attachment that I've never felt before. I've certainly never had feelings for a man on this scale before. I've never let myself.

He was this distant object of desire. I've had a thing for him for a long time. A very long time.

And there was something about that that kept me safe. When it was a theory. And then I kept myself even safer by making him my enemy. I kept all my intense feelings bottled up, and found boys my own age who didn't challenge me, who didn't like me on fire.

Being with him, it's reaching for the sun. For an object that might scald me. For something that I never wanted to let myself have. Being with him is incredible.

He's so far beyond any fantasy I ever dared to have.

We sit down in the grass, and I set the basket out. I brought a small blanket, not for us to sit on, but to put the Tupperware on, because the idea of putting it straight on the grass just feels a little bit too close to nature for me.

Ants can stay well away from my picnic.

I'm happier to focus on that than I am on my current emotional state. I wait for conversation to strike up easily between us. It doesn't. That's unusual. I can't tell if it's me or if it's him. "You didn't even have trouble sitting down," I point out. Mainly because I'm desperate to get something going, but I'm not sure that was the right thing to say.

He looks at his crutches. "No. I didn't. Sometimes I don't even think that much about it anymore."

"Because whatever happens, you're just going to keep... Being you. Figuring it out."

"I guess that's life. Isn't it? I mean, you've been through some stuff, but you just keep on doing it."

"Yeah," I say.

I have a feeling that he's going to go on the list of things I've been through. I don't think that drawing a boundary around this and forgetting it happened is going to be easy. Hell, I'm tempted to say that it will even be possible. But I can't think that way. We jumped into this, and we need to be able to get back out of it. For the sake of our family. For our sake.

I've heard the term forest bathing before, but never thought much about it. As I sit there beneath the pine trees, the sun pouring down on me, I feel like I understand it. Like there's something healing out here. A baptism among the firs, and he's with me for it. With me in it.

Then, he reaches across the distance and touches my face. I recognize that look on his face. Intense, longing.

"This is literally a public space."

"There's no one here," he says.

I've never been as attracted to anyone as I am to this man. I've never wanted somebody so badly that I was willing to take a risk like this. He makes me want to do it.

He makes me want to forget everything, drop all my rules, drop all my worries, and embrace him.

And why not? If he's going to be a hard learned lesson, if I'm already sleeping with my stepbrother, then I might as well take this risk. It might as well be him and me, here under the sky, with the trees as witnesses, and all that healing sun. It might as well be as dirty and brilliant and risky as all that.

Because maybe healing has to hurt.

God knows his is.

Maybe the kind I need to do is going to hurt too. I never really thought about it. About all the ways that I've been protecting myself. I thought that I had processed my mom's death. As well as you can, anyway.

It's not like I would've chosen it, but I feel a certain sort of peace.

But... Do I? Or do I just hold parts of myself back so that I'm never really hurt. Do I keep from challenging those tender places? Those parts of me that are vulnerable and raw.

He doesn't wait for me to say yes. He kisses me. There's a desperation to it. A deep sort of longing. As if he senses the magnitude of the moment too. Maybe he's thinking about the end, just like I am. Or maybe he's just thinking about this and us and the whole sky bearing witness.

I can't say.

I'm not sure that it matters. We are experiencing this intensity together, and I find there's something beautiful in that. Hell, it's been beautiful the whole time. That we both want this. Beyond reason, madness and anything else. I give myself over to the kiss. Open my mouth wide so he can take it deep. His hands move over my body, effortlessly removing my dress. I strip his shirt away, push him onto his back. I want him. I need him.

We're always responsible. We always use condoms.

But I'm on the pill, and I feel a risky edge to this that I want to explore. Like I want to stop shielding myself, and feel everything. I want him inside me with nothing between us. I have never wanted that before. In fact, I would say that I wanted the condom. I wanted a barrier between myself and the man that I was having sex with, and if that doesn't say something about those relationships, nothing else can.

But suddenly, I need him. I crave him. Want to be filled with him.

Is that twisted? Maybe.

I'm there. Twisted, undone. For him.

Only for him. I want to give him everything. I want to lay it all down. I want to be more vulnerable. Is that even possible? Like we only have this very limited amount of time, and I need to experience the full extent of all the feelings that can exist between us. I have to.

I'm not gentle when I tear at his belt, his jeans, until he's free.

"It's okay," I say, throwing my leg over him and taking him deep inside of me.

"Hell," he breathes, as he enters me slowly. I feel each excruciating edge of him keenly. I moan, his hot, bare skin driving me insane.

He starts to arch his hips upward, claiming me, fucking me with an intensity that shocks me. I didn't know that he could do that from this position, especially not with his injuries, but Lord. He's taking me to another planet.

He takes me like that, over and over again while I arch my hips and ride along with the rhythm. It's fast, it's furious, and he comes in a hot rush inside of me. Making me tremble, shake, cry out his name.

And as the echo of our voices fades into the trees, I realize that we've just taken a massive risk.

I can't bring myself to care. To be regretful. To be embarrassed.

"That was amazing," he says.

"I've never..." I collapse onto his chest for a moment, before sliding off of him. "I've never done that before. Without a condom."

He shakes his head. "Me neither."

"Really? Never?"

"No. I... Generally speaking I would rather double up than ever forget. You know how my dad is. I've always been clear that I was never going to litter the world with my bastards." He's quiet for a moment. "If you got pregnant I'd take care of you. I would take care of the baby."

That quiet admission, the fact that he would take on that kind of responsibility just because we both lost control, makes my heart squeeze tight.

"I'm on the pill," I say. "So, that's not going to happen. I just... I don't usually do that, because it seems to... Close."

But it didn't this time?

"No," I say. "It felt right. It felt good."

He touches my cheek. "I kind of like it that you thought about it."

"You thought I did it on accident? I said it was okay."

"Yeah. But I sure as hell wasn't thinking. But I just kind of like that you did. That you actually just wanted me. Like that."

And I liked it that he hadn't thought of it all. That he lost control. We might be opposites, but we are apparently kind of mutually needy and messed up.

Good thing we have those boundaries.

Good thing.

"This is by far my favorite trip to the lake that I've ever had."

I laugh, my voice echoing across the water. "Me too. But you know, we're going to have to figure out how to act around other people."

He nods slowly. "Yeah. You think that bar night is a great idea?"

"Yeah. Sure. I think it's a good idea. Because that's going to be life, isn't it? After this is all over."

"Yeah," he says. "It is."

We've never been awkward after sex, not even really the first time. But for some reason, this time feels a little bit awkward. I wonder if it's just having to come down from the intensity of it. I know I personally had some big realizations in the lead up to it. I don't know if he did.

I want to ask, but I'm not brave enough. This is so tangled up. And it hasn't felt tangled up, not the whole time. It's felt great. Good and fine.

But now suddenly it feels a little bit fraught.

I've never had a relationship before. Not a real one. I've never felt like I couldn't dig or ask for what the guy was thinking or feeling. Because I've never worried what he might have to say. The stakes just never felt all that high.

And suddenly, with him, I feel terrified. Just really terrified. For the first time in a couple of weeks, I excuse myself to go home. I need distance. A break. My own bed.

He fires up a group text, with Dallas and Sarah, Gentry and Lily and me.

> Everyone free to go to the saloon tomorrow night? I'm feeling adventurous.

There's a round of enthusiastic agreements. I give it a thumbs up, because I'm feeling a little bit muted, even in the text conversation. Tomorrow we're going to go out and pretend that nothing's going on. It's important, I know it is.

But for some reason, it mainly feels like the beginning of the end.

Chapter Thirteen

Colt

I can't stop thinking about how distant Allison seemed after the lake yesterday. I also don't like how empty my bed was last night, I don't like how empty it was this morning, and I don't like drinking coffee by myself. I know she has a shift at the store today, but I still think she should've stayed with me. She's done it other nights when she had work.

I hear myself in my own head. I'm whiny, and I'm pouting. I haven't been this bad since... Well, I was going to say early on in the injury, but really, it's just been since I've been sharing space with her. Everything has felt more doable. Everything has felt easier.

Going out tonight doesn't feel easy. For a number of reasons. One of them being that Allison and I have to pretend that nothing is happening. Because I can't even imagine the trauma if our small town found out what we were doing. Much less the issues that it would create in the family. It's not even fun to imagine as a bit. It's just a horror.

But I'm also not looking forward to tonight because this is me, stepping out as healed as I am, as healed as I'm not, I'm so used to just being... The version of myself that I was. I guess I'm still him in a lot of ways. I still feel ambition. The desire to go back to the rodeo, to ride. Though there is a dark cloud over that. The anxiety that I feel when I think about the accident. Yeah. I need to deal with that. I need to see a therapist, probably. Weird realization to have as I'm getting ready to go out to a bar.

Or maybe it's not. I don't want to be my dad. I don't know my dad's life story, honestly. I don't know that I need to. He definitely doesn't seem like a man who has ever healed from a single thing. Maybe he's just a narcissist. Maybe he just runs around hurting people because. Or maybe it's because there were things that were done to him that were wrong too. And he's just paying it forward. I feel like you actually have to do some work to not pay your hurt forward. As epiphanies go, I don't necessarily find this to be a welcome one. But it makes me feel like this pursuit of not being my father might be winnable in ways I hadn't realized. Because I can make a choice. Because I can take steps, action toward not being him.

Maybe I should talk to Allison about that. About the fact that I need to see a therapist.

I look at myself in the mirror. Me from a couple of months ago would've thought that this was weak. Admitting that I need some help. I don't see it that way now. It's like something has shifted inside of me.

It's not weak to ask for help.

Strong people do it.

I saw my injured body as something weak, something wrong, but my body is strong. It survived. It's like this, in a way that I would describe as being not perfect, but it's mine.

Maybe I'll never be able to do everything that I could before. I can have sex with Allison. Give her pleasure. I can go to the lake. I can go out to a bar.

I'm alive.

And that's something to be grateful for. Bodies are difficult. They can turn on you. Disease can eat them from the inside.

But mine saved me. I swallow hard, and walk out of the bathroom, head into the living room. I put on one boot. I get up on my crutches. I text Allison.

You almost ready?

Yes.

She comes to the door two minutes later, wearing a white sundress that makes me want to thump my foot and howl like a cartoon wolf. I'm never going to be able to be normal about her again. She's so sexy. I've always thought so. But I could put that away. I could minimize it. I can't now. Now every time I look at her, I'm going to be looking right through whatever she's wearing. I'm going to have a detailed impression of her gorgeous body burned into my mind. I am so, so profoundly screwed.

"You look great," I say, my voice sounding rougher than I intended it to.

"So do you," she says.

I think I look ridiculous. With my cut-up jeans and my giant brace. My black T-shirt and my black cowboy hat, like I'm still some kind of bad son of a bitch.

But it's nice of her to say.

I've never had a fragile ego. It's always been very, very healthy. But it's taken a little bit of a beating the last month and a half.

And anyway, it means something different to hear it from her.

"Let's go," she says.

We get into the car and she drives us the short distance to the saloon. We have to park around the corner, all the way up the curb, and she looks at me apologetically.

"Sorry. Kind of a long walk."

"No longer than the walk to the lake." I look at her. "You okay?"

She looks away. "Yeah."

I reach out and grip her chin, turning her face toward me. "Something's bothering you."

"It's not. It's really not."

"Don't bullshit me, Allison. You've never been especially good at it, and now I know you way too well."

"It's... It's just that yesterday was really intense. I'm afraid that I don't know quite what to do with it. I don't really know how to handle it."

"You don't have to do anything. It's just us."

"But not tonight. Tonight it's not just us. Tonight we have to go in there and... Pretend nothing's happening."

"It's fine," I say. "Listen, we're friends." I hear the words come out of my mouth, and I don't like them. I don't feel like they're exactly right. And yet, I say them anyway. "We're always going to be friends after this. And we're going to have nights like this. This thing between you and me, we'll always have that. But it shouldn't hurt. Or be hard or scary. We'll just lean into the friendship part in there. It'll be fine."

I can't say for sure that I believe all that. She looked so sad, and I don't know what else to do. I want to talk to her about therapy. I want to have her to myself tonight, but I can't. Everything's going to be okay. Something about the intensity of the lake bothered her. It was intense. It was amazing. I've never been with anybody without a condom, and it was...

I push the thought away. We have to go be in public now.

I get out of the car, and begin my trudge up the sidewalk. At our home – *my* house. Weird that I'm thinking of it that way in context with her – we hold hands a lot. But that's not going to happen here. I walk into the bar, with her behind me. And I don't think I was adequately prepared for the force of everyone looking at me when I walk in. I feel a little bit less like a narcissist when I feel the wave of reaction that goes through the room.

I'm not making it up. People around here definitely have opinions about me.

"Colt!" Laz throws his hands up from behind the bar, a wide smile on his face. "Your drinks are on me tonight."

"You have to do that," I say.

"If they're not on him, they're on me," says an older, grizzled rancher, who I think is named Mark, sitting at the end of the bar.

"No, drinks are definitely on me."

I blink hard when I see Dane Parker getting up and walking toward me. He has a slight limp. From the exact same sort of accident that I was in. "From one busted-up bull rider to another, please let me get drinks for you and your whole party."

"That's... That's too kind of you." Dane was one of the men who taught me to ride. Him and Dallas's dad Bennett. I haven't seen Dane in a long time.

"I'd get a drink with you, but my wife is antsy to leave."

His wife, Beatrix, smiles a few tables away. I've always

thought she was really pretty. A redhead. Maybe I have a thing for redheads.

"We have to get home to the kids," she says. "And Evan."

"Evan is still alive?" Evan is a rescue raccoon that Beatrix has had for years, and he's mildly famous around town.

"Yes," she says. "A raccoon's life expectancy is pretty short when they're in the wild left to their own devices, but since Evan domesticated himself, he's living fat and happy in the house."

"In the *house*," Dane says. "This is my life." But he looks happy. "Women will do that to you. Love does that to you."

He found love after his accident.

He also never went back to the rodeo. For some reason, I think maybe I can be okay with that. I think I have to be. Whatever the outcome is, I think I have to be okay with the possibility that I might not go back. I might not be able to. I might not want to.

"Thanks again," I say.

He tips his hat, smiles and walks out with his wife.

"A pet raccoon," I say as Allison approaches me. "That's the weirdest thing."

"That was nice of him," she says.

"Yeah. Really nice."

The door opens again, and Dallas, Sarah, Lily and Gentry walk into the bar. "This is like that scene in The Lord of the Rings when Frodo wakes up in the house of Elrond and is reunited with everyone," Sarah says after we greet each other enthusiastically.

Dallas looks at her. "I don't think anyone else knows what that is."

"I do," Gentry says.

We stop cluttering up the front of the bar, and head back to the back of the bar. We had Sarah's birthday party here last year. It's funny how much things can change. I was on top of my game. Hitting on her with actually no insight into her relationship with Dallas. Dancing like nothing on my body could ever hurt ever. It's funny, though. Because I've always felt untouchable.

But that means more than one thing. I always felt like there was a certain amount of security in my position. But I've also always felt distant. From a lot of people in my life. Like there's some deep part of me that nobody really touches. Everybody gets the performance. Nobody gets me.

That feels safest. It feels like the right thing. The only thing.

It feels like what I have to do to survive.

I push that thought away, because it doesn't belong here tonight. It doesn't belong here when we're trying to have a good time. When I'm trying to have a reentry. If I wanted to navel gaze, I could do that at home. Hell. I've been doing it. I don't need to do it here.

That round of drinks arrives, and Allison gets a daiquiri. I replay memories of being in this bar, when she wasn't mine.

Mine.

She's not mine. Not really. Even if I could claim her publicly, I can't...

I decide not to think about that too deeply. There's no point. Not really. It is what it is. We're stuck in this high-stakes poker game that we shouldn't have started playing to begin with. But we did. Because we did, we have to deal with the discomfort. Because we did, I have to deal with this strange, crushing sensation in my chest that makes me want her to be mine, but I also know that she can't be.

Gentry would kill me. If he had any idea what I was doing to his sister.

To *my stepsister*.

There are layers to how bad of an idea this was, and yet here we are. We use that sex logic to get us all the way here, and now I have to sit in the discomfort of it. That was one thing in the bubble. Sitting in my house, cocooned by how different everything was. Dragging it out into this familiar space, with other people around, that's a lot different. Yeah. It's a hell of a lot different.

I try to look at her like I would have a few months ago. I try to look at this like I would have a few months ago. A year ago. We've gone out together so many times. Usually, she and I are not drawn to each other. Usually, there's something that keeps us apart. I know what it is now. It isn't just a casual forbidden attraction on my part.

A chemical sleeper agent that had been waiting for the right reactor to get added to it. My accident. Us getting too close. Us spending so much time together.

Now it's exploded into something I can't control.

Apparently, that's why I was keeping my distance, always. Not just because of the way she treated me.

She was smart, though.

She always knew what *could* happen.

At some point, the music gets turned up so loud it's deafening. And somebody switches it to seriously old-school country. There is a lot of yelling about me, my recovery, my heroism – somehow? I think it's a little bit much, but I also feel... Like it's something normal. Something mine.

I stopped thinking about Allison. I start imagining being

myself again. Going back to the rodeo. Making it to the championship. If I can do that...

If I can do that, then I can still...

It matters to me. It matters to me a hell of a lot.

I want to win. Everything. I want to prove to my dad that he was wrong about me. I want to do what he couldn't do himself. I want to prove to everyone in this town that their love for me isn't unfounded. I can be everything they ever imagined I could be. I'm the guy. The one.

It's not a burden. It's something that I cultivated.

Because Gold Valley has been good to me. And if I'm going to be its favorite son, then I need to be worthy of that.

I feel it right now, maybe it's the beer, maybe it's the whiskey that I added on top of that. Allison has been nursing a daiquiri slowly. She has to drive us home, so I know she has to go extremely light on the alcohol. I almost feel bad. Almost.

But this is my party. It didn't start that way, but it turned into it.

I relish this moment to just not be in complicated thought patterns. To not worry.

Maybe I can just forget that anything has changed. Yeah, I have a big brace on my leg, but everything else feels normal. Maybe it can be a year ago in my mind. When my life hadn't changed. When everything felt all right.

Then I look up, over at the back of the bar, and I see a man talking to Allison. He reaches out, touches her cheek, and she lowers her eyes. And suddenly, I'm not seeing this bar through the haze of alcohol. Through the delightful haze of a party. No. Suddenly, all I see is red.

I walk over to where she is, and practically get between them. "Move along. She doesn't want to talk to you."

She looks at me. "Colt. I've got it."

"He looks like he's bothering you."

"He's not bothering me."

"He should be," I say, feeling a rush of rage that I know I have no entitlement to. I was just thinking about how everything could be back the way that it was. How everything could be normal again. And here I am, doing something I would never have done before.

Allison is beautiful. Men flirt with her. It's something that happens all the time. And it's definitely not something I'm entitled to manage. I know that. But I can't stand there and watch this while she's mine. She's been in my bed for weeks now. My bed. And maybe she isn't going to stay there. Hell, I don't think anyone is going to be a permanent fixture there. That's for other men. Other men who...

It doesn't matter why. It doesn't matter. She's mine right now.

"Isn't she your stepsister?" The guy is clearly picking up on the holy-shit-so-inappropriate jealousy radiating off of me in waves, and I can't even care.

"Yeah. She is. Don't go getting on a girl in front of her brother."

"Oh Jesus Christ," Allison says, turning away from me and from him and stalking across the bar toward Gentry and Lily.

Okay. I think I messed up. I caused a little bit more of a scene than I anticipated. I definitely made her unhappy.

"She's just... Not in the place to get hit on right now," I say, a weird, half-assed, slightly drunk attempt at covering for what I just did.

When I come back over to the table, everyone is looking at me. Except for Allison.

No one has the guts to say anything, though.

"It's a party," I say. "Everybody, stop looking so serious."

Which is when I just start drinking more. Because I don't want to feel anything. I don't want to feel the conflicting emotions that are rolling around inside of me. I don't want to deal with any of this.

The atmosphere is celebratory, but I'm not anymore. I fake it. Because God, dammit, if there's one thing I'm really good at, it's smiling. All the damned time. Being the golden retriever that everybody wants me to be. I am so good at that. I would probably fetch a ball if they asked me to. Look at me.

Which is right about the time I decide that I'm going to walk home.

Gentry and Lily are already collecting all their things, Dallas and Sarah left 30 minutes before, and Allison is looking sulky and sober in the corner.

"I need some fresh air. I'm going to walk back."

"You are not," Allison says.

"Yes I am," I growl.

"You're not," she says.

"You're not the boss of me," I say, the incredibly inelegant playground retort about the only thing that's rolling effortlessly off my tongue right now.

The bar has more or less emptied out, and most people are a little bit too lost in the sauce to see me storm heavily through the building on my crutches and out the front door.

Once I'm on the sidewalk, I sincerely regret my choices, but still make my way down the block toward the cross street that'll take me back to my house.

My whole head feels too hot. My body feels like it's on fire. I don't like anything about what happened in there.

About how it made me feel. About how I showed my hands to other people there. I just don't like it. That's not who I am. I'm not jealous. I have no right to be jealous of some guy with her. If I can't control myself even in that environment...

I hear the sound of a truck on the road behind me, and I turn. It's Allison, in the driver's seat, moving slowly behind me in the street.

Then she pulls up beside me and rolls down the window. "What are you doing?"

"Getting some air."

"You're being stupid," she says. "Get in the truck. Don't overtax yourself. You already drank too much, and you're honestly just being an asshole."

"I'm not an asshole," I say. "Everybody likes me."

"I don't like you very much right now."

"I don't care."

"Fine. You don't care what I think. Just what everybody else thinks. That's great, Colt. Just get in the truck."

I just want to push back against everything and everyone. I hate this. Because everything is bad. Absolutely everything. And things were better a year ago. I've never felt that way before in my life. I always felt like I was making progress. I always felt like life got better, like I got better the older I got, the closer I got to the championship, the further away I got from the little boy who was abandoned by his father. Everything got better. Now it's all crashed down around me. Nothing is better. Nothing.

I look at her. Her face.

And something moves in my chest. I don't like that either. Because it's dark and intense, and it is whispering things to me that I don't want to deal with. I don't want to translate them. I don't want to dig deep.

I didn't use to have to do that.

"I want to deal with it," I say. And I realize she's not in my head, and that she has no idea what I'm talking about, but it's what I say out loud anyway.

"And I don't want to babysit you. I don't want to deal with the questions that I'm going to get from Sarah after tonight. You know exactly what you look like, don't you?"

"Like a jealous guy who's fucking you," I growl.

"Get in the car, Colt Campbell, you are standing in the street yelling about... Get in the car."

Finally, that's the one thing that gets me to do it. Also, I'm tired.

I'm miserable. I think I might be crashing out. How have I made it this long without totally crashing out?

Maybe because I can almost see the light at the end of the tunnel. Maybe because I was somewhere normal, getting treated like I was me, and I just still don't feel like me.

All the coping strategies that have carried me through my life don't seem to be working right now. Which just really sucks.

I close the passenger door, and then she drives away from the curb, the trip home taking two minutes. She doesn't say anything to me.

"Sober up. We'll deal with each other later."

"There's nothing to deal with. I could tell you didn't want him to talk to you, so I don't know why you're pissed I stopped it from happening."

"I didn't especially want to talk to him, no. I wasn't exactly open to flirting tonight. But I can also handle myself, and I don't need you running around acting like you're jealous when we both know you're not. You were happy to ignore me for most of the evening. You only know how to have sex with me, or treat me like you used to. This is why I was smart to... I knew the picnic was weird. An anomaly. It felt kind of romantic. But we are not that. I see that. I get it. We are not romantic. But that means that it's just sex, and it's just more of the same when we're out in public, and I don't like that. It made me feel gross. Especially when you acted possessive, when we both know that's about my body and not about anything else. I just don't need this."

I know that I should say something. Something to make her feel better, but I don't know what to say. She's not wrong. It is the only thing I know how to do. I know how to be with her when we're by ourselves. I know how to strip her naked, how to make her scream my name. I even know how to hold her afterward. But I didn't know how to be anywhere near her tonight without touching her. So maybe that's on me. Maybe this is something messed up inside of me.

Something broken. But what other option is there? We are stepsiblings. We've addressed this. We can't take it out of that private space. She knows that, so do I. But I get that it feels bad. Because I feel bad.

But I don't have anything to say, so I just maneuver myself out of the vehicle, into my driveway, and head into the house.

I don't go to bed, I lie down on the couch. I try to figure out something to say to her tomorrow. But I don't know what to say.

This is another thing I don't like about any of the changes that have happened. I feel helpless.

I've deliberately made a life where I don't feel that way.

And now I do. Pretty much all the time.

It's unbearable.

And the only thing that ever made all this bearable was having Allison here with me.

Tonight, she isn't here.

She probably won't be again.

I probably messed it up. And that hurts worse than my leg has for a good while.

Chapter Fourteen

Allison

The dinner invitation from my dad is unwelcome. Mainly because I don't want to see anybody right now, much less my family, much less difficult. We've made a lot of excuses the last few weeks to not do that together, and I have a feeling it's not going to wash. Not after last night, not with Gentry and Lily there.

I know that I need to go and talk to Colt. But I've been avoiding him the whole day for pretty good reason.

I've just about got my motivation to go and talk to him when there's a knock on my door.

I know it's him. I feel a little bit satisfied by that. Because apparently he feels bad about all this too. Last night I questioned that. Whether or not we really have the connection that it felt like we did for the last few weeks. Part of me would love to be satisfied by his jealousy, but it's not an emotional jealousy.

It was possessiveness.

It was about my physical body, not about me as a person.

I just know that. I don't need to deep dive into the whiskey-drunk mind of Colt Campbell to know that. Especially given the way he treated me the entire night. Like he didn't have anything to say to me, like there was no expanding and deepening relationship between the two of us, which nobody would be that surprised by. I've been taking care of him for the last three weeks. You would expect that we would maybe have a little bit more of an understanding between us than we did before.

He's a mess.

Maybe I am too. Because I told myself that I was going to keep my emotions in order if we did this. I told myself it was going to help me through the unrequited feelings I've had for him for years. Instead, I've been straying into dangerous territory. Essentially, I've been pushing through an injury rather than letting it heal. Emotionally, I'm Colt. I jerk the door open, and there he is.

"I need to talk to you," he says.

"Yeah. I was about to come talk to you. My dad invited us over for dinner."

He nods. "I know. I also got a text. But that's not what I want to talk to you about. I'm sorry about last night. I was drunk."

"I know you were. But I also think that maybe there was a lot of truth in the things that you said."

He looks a little bit blank. "I'll be honest with you. I'm not entirely sure what I said, and what was just me ranting in my head."

"You said enough, but I'm sure there was a little bit that you kept on the inside. And you know what? You're welcome to go ahead and keep it on the inside."

"I'm sorry," he says.

"I know you are. You never want to hurt me or anyone. Last night you were who you aspire to be. Except when you got in that dude's face."

"I just... I know that you're mad at me about the way that I treated you last night, but the honest truth is, I don't know how to be near you without... Touching you." He looks undone by that admission. A little bit helpless, and I feel something inside me soften. To me, that felt like a rejection of myself, my whole self, as a human being. Maybe I'm looking at it the wrong way. Maybe I'm not being entirely fair. I've had years of practice with wanting him and not showing it. I thought it might be nice to sit and act like friends actually in a public space.

Or maybe I'm just naïve. Naïve to think that at the end of all of this we can come out in a better place than we went in.

But it didn't feel like it was unreasonable. And I felt wounded, like if I wasn't naked he didn't need me. Which is a progression. Because for a bit I didn't care about that. When we started, I told myself that all that mattered was that it was my fantasy. It didn't matter what his feelings were. Now, I feel like his feelings do matter, and that scares me.

"I wasn't trying to hurt you. I was trying to act right, and then I didn't. I know I didn't. I screwed up. You were talking to that other guy, and I just got upset. I get that I don't really have the right to do that. I don't know what I'm doing." He closes his eyes. "I just want to go back. To the way things were before. Not you specifically. My life. When things weren't complicated I always knew what I wanted. I always knew what I was doing."

"You always knew what you wanted?" I try to keep the

edge of bitterness out of my voice. "What must that be like? I guess you have to be uncertain like the rest of us now."

"Why are you mad at me?"

"I don't actually know." It's as honest as I can be. Because what do I want from him? Do I want him to scoop me up in a crowd of people and acknowledge me? Am I angry that he didn't display perfect friendship with me? Am I angry that he was jealous, and might have betrayed what's happening between us to the people we are closest to, which will bring it out in the open and force us to deal with things, and if we have to do that, I'll feel... What? Embarrassed? Ashamed? The trouble is, I don't actually know. And I'm expecting him to know. I'm expecting him to handle all of this perfectly in ways that I'm certainly not.

I'm feeling far, far too much. That's all I know.

He was just the one who got jealous. If some woman had talked to him, and I was right there, I don't know what I would've done.

And all of it is especially pointless because we can't make this anything. I just feel helpless and angry about it. I just feel more than I want to, and maybe none of it's a good idea. But the idea of calling it off, of not being with him for the next month – we have a month – hurts me. I want to be with him. I want to spend the summer with him. So maybe I'm the problem, and maybe I need to figure out how to just accept this. It seems like something I should know how to do.

How to accept losing something that I wish that I could keep. That's life. Nothing is permanent. Nothing lasts. Not really. Every day you're one step closer to losing more people in your life, to losing relationships, to people leaving your life as quickly as they came into it.

I know that. I've known it since I was a kid.

Something about the feelings I have for Colt stands in opposition to that. They want to be part of who I am. Grafted into my bones. I don't want to love him.

Because it's impossible.

Maybe that's the problem. We had one moment last night where things felt a little bit real, and it was the wrong thing. He wasn't supposed to be possessive of me, and the truth is, I liked it. The truth is, I wish he would've been more possessive. Wish he would've kissed me. Wish he would've claimed me in front of everybody. He didn't. He stopped himself.

I guess the problem is me.

"There's no reason for us to fight about this. It was a weird night. It was your first time out since the accident, and things are weird with us."

"Weird? That's one way to put it."

"It's about the nicest way that I can put it."

"What's the point of being nice?"

"I know you're not suggesting we aim for honesty over niceness. I don't think either of us actually wants that."

"Okay, how's this for honesty? I think I need therapy."

I can only stare at him. Shocked. "You... You what?"

"I don't want to be like my dad."

"You're not like your dad."

"I am. You saw me last night. Possessive. Selfish. Self-aggrandizing. The attention suits me just fine. *He's* like that, and I've done my level best not to hurt people with that. But I hurt you."

"It's not that simple."

"What isn't?"

"What exactly hurt me. I don't even know how to articulate it. I just know that everything inside of me felt gross. I'm not actually sure it's your fault. I certainly don't want you to use it as evidence that you're a narcissist of some kind."

"I just want to be better at relationships, then. I'm good at... That. I'm good in a crowd. This one-on-one stuff, I don't really know how to do it. Even my friendship with Gentry and Dallas, it kind of hinges on it being all of us. In different combinations. At the rodeo we hang out with this girl, Stella. She's a barrel racer. The more people I can have around me, the better I do. The shallower everything is, and... You're right. About the fact that I don't know how to just sit and talk to you. Not all the time. We've done a little bit of that, and it's good. But it's also out of the ordinary for me. And I definitely don't know how to integrate it into being at a bar. Being on the Gold Valley stage. So to speak. I feel like I belong to everybody else, and not really to me. And I wonder if that's... I don't know my dad, really. So all I can do is guess. But I want to get down to the bottom of why I am the way I am."

"You just told me that you don't like the way that everything has changed."

"It's complicated." He smiles at me ruefully.

"Maybe you needed to go through all the changes to get to this one."

He grimaces. "Probably."

Just like I think I need to get a good look at what a mess he is up close. To see how wonderful and terrible this thing between us can be. If nothing else, I've learned some things about myself. About how intense physical attraction can be for me.

I'm definitely not going to sleep with just *some guy* again if I don't have this. Why would I? Maybe knowing that I can have it is the first step. And I hate the idea of Colt being a training ground for anything, just the same as I hate the idea that I've been some kind of emotional training ground for him. That him not knowing what to do with me is pushing him to make changes so that he can be better for somebody else.

But the reality of who we are to each other means that's just how it has to be.

There is no other alternative.

I can accept this. And I can accept that whatever happens, it's going to be okay, because I can choose to learn from it, to grow from it. Just like the other bad things I've been through. This doesn't have to be a bad thing.

I got a little bit too deep without remembering that this is going to end.

I loved my mom, even knowing I was going to lose her. I can give myself over to this thing, knowing that it's going to end. Accepting that it's going to end. It's one of the things that my experiences have prepared me for. If I am going to be a good nurse. You have to be pragmatic. Not emotional, it's what I've always done. It's why I distanced Colt in the first place, and now I've made a different decision, and I'm going to have to accept that position.

"So. Dinner tonight."

He nods slowly. "Dinner tonight."

Chapter Fifteen

Colt

She drives us tonight, and it's strange walking up to the house together, but separate. It's sort of like last night, but in a more profound way.

We sort of settled things earlier.

We shared some things.

I crashed out, and I'm having to climb up out of that, but I can. I've made a decision. And that's good. I don't want to be like my dad. I don't want to be forever chasing the spotlight because I don't know how to be without it.

I don't want to be a narcissist. It's not enough anymore to just avoid having certain attachments so that I don't hurt people. I want to actually change. And if I had to bottom out to come to that realization, then fine. It's fine.

What I've learned is that rock-bottom isn't the place I hit in that arena. It's contending with everything afterward. With not knowing what to do when life doesn't obey me.

When I can't manipulate a situation with charm. When I can't force my body to heal faster than it's going to.

When I can't just decide to be healed.

She's right. It's probably something I need to go through. It's clearly something my dad never went through, and he made the decision to not be changed or affected by having a son. I need to make a different decision.

That's all really clear to me now. The healing journey isn't just sitting around letting my bones knit themselves back together. It's also getting on top of myself. Not just drinking to deal with pain that I actually need to be able to face head-on.

We receive a warm greeting from everybody in the house, though Gentry is measured.

Lily isn't here tonight, which is unusual.

"She has a date," he says casually.

"A date?"

I haven't really known Lily to date. Partly because she so... Obsessed with Gentry.

"Yeah. A date." I watch his face to see if he has any emotions about it, but he's unreadable. Gentry can be like that.

Allison has shared more with me in the last few weeks about the impact of her mom's death, and about her memories surrounding her, than Gentry has in the last ten years. He's just not that kind of person.

"Well. Good luck to her I guess."

That does earn me an expression I can't quite read. But then we are having steak and corn on the cob, baked potatoes and one of my stepdad's great pies. So I'm not thinking about anything else for a moment. Good food, good family. This house. It's a home, in a way that nothing else ever really has been for me.

These people are my home.

When dinner finishes, Allison is quick to volunteer to do dishes, and I'm about to do the same when Gentry jabbed me in the shoulder. "I need to talk to you."

My stomach tightens. "Do you?"

"Outside."

I already know what it's about. I don't need him to give me a knowing look, or explain anything. I just know.

We head out the back door, and I'm hoping that we don't attract attention. I'm bracing myself. For him to yell at me. For him to punch me in my face. For him to sit me down and interrogate me like I'm a criminal.

I'd deserve any of those things.

I knew that I had messed up last night. And I had a very strong feeling that Gentry had seen it. I was hoping, since he didn't storm my front door early in the morning that it meant I had gotten away with it. But apparently not.

"So, what do you need to tell me?"

I think about trying to get around it. About making him say at first. Because if he doesn't know, and I tell him, I'm just causing drama that doesn't need to exist.

But I already know.

And one part of my realization from my collapse last night is that I have to own my shit. I have to stand there and take it on the chin, maybe literally.

"I'm sleeping with your sister."

I expect Gentry to lunge forward. Instead, he lets out a slow breath, rocks back on his heels, and drags his hand down over his face. "All right. Okay. You're sleeping with her."

"Yeah. I am."

"To what end?"

"To no end, Gentry. We just... I don't know. It was a

forced proximity or something." The lie tastes bitter on my tongue. Forced proximity, a whole lot of longing that boiled over and had to express itself. One or the other.

The fact that she's beautiful and smart and resilient. The fact that she has shown me so many things about how to be a better person. How to be a more accepting, together person. The fact that I'm just saying I'm sleeping with her rather than in a relationship with her, but it's not a relationship. Not really. It also isn't just sex. But just like last night at the bar, I don't know how to express that.

"We didn't want anyone to know, because we're aware that it's messed."

"Okay, let's start over. You and Allison are sleeping together."

"Correct."

"But that's all it is."

"Yes. She's going to move closer to the hospital in a couple of months. I don't know if she's talked to you about that. But it makes more sense for rotations and all of that. So..."

"So, distance is the problem?"

I laughed. "No. The problem is that she's my stepsister. You know how everybody in town would react to that."

"Who cares? You're Colt Campbell. You can do whatever you want. You could do the electric slide naked down Main Street, and people would be like: Wow, that's a really cool thing he's doing. Why do you think anyone would care if you were with her?"

"Don't be dense. You know how it looks. It looks like maybe... I don't know. Like something happened when we lived together, and it didn't."

"I know it didn't. I know you. I don't think that you ever took advantage of my teenage sister when we lived together.

I don't think you ever used your position as her stepbrother to do anything inappropriate. If I thought you would do that, I wouldn't be your friend, Colt."

The way he says that, so incredulous, so intense, feels like a shotgun blast to my chest. He's not getting mad at me. I really expected him to. I expected him to tell me but I'm an asshole for touching her. For corrupting her. For using her while I am recovering. He's not doing it.

"But people might think that."

"I don't think so. You don't have a reputation for ever doing anything like that. I just... What I actually wanted to tell you is that I think you guys are good together."

"What?"

"I know. But that's why I sat on this ever since I noticed that things were off between you guys. And I've been noticing it. But last night confirmed it. I knew there was more going on than either of you was indicating. She... Colt, she's in love with you."

Everything inside of me freezes. "What?"

"She's in love with you, man. She always has been. She thinks the sun rises and sets on you. And you... You're a good guy. She's dated so many losers. And I hate every single one of them."

"You're supposed to... You're supposed to punch me. And tell me that I'm not good enough for her. Tell me that I can't corrupt her like this."

"I'm under no illusions that my sister's a virgin of any kind, and you're not using her, are you?"

"No. I'm not. But I... I'm not using her."

"I know. I don't know why you think that it has to end. I think you should try. That's what I wanted to tell you. But I want you to give it an actual try. And if you need my help smoothing it over with Dad and Cindy..."

"No, Gentry. I don't. Because she needs to finish nursing school, and I need to get my ship together. I've got to go back to the rodeo, I've got to win the championship. I can't be in a relationship. Not right now. I'm... I'm too messed up. I'm too dysfunctional, and she doesn't deserve that."

"I'm not friends with a dysfunctional person."

"I hate to break it to you, you are. I put on a good front, but I'm afraid I'm more like my dad than my mom, and when the rubber meets the road, I am not the kind of guy that you want your sister to be shackled to for the rest of her life. Trust me on this."

"How would you know? You've never tried. You keep yourself so... So emotionally separate from everyone and everything. And I see something in the two of you. I feel like she's the person who can actually reach you. Hell, some guy talking to her last night rattled the hell out of you. And I kind of like that, Colt. I like you having to fight for it. I'm not glad that you're hurt, but at the same time, I think this might have been what you needed. I want to see you dig deep for something."

"I'm almost a fucking rodeo champion, Gentry, it's not like I don't dig deep or work hard."

"I never said you didn't work hard. But everything you do, all your achievements, all of that, tell me that's not just you putting your accolades between you and other people so that you don't have to have actual emotions."

"Fuck you."

"That's how it's going to be? You're going to admit that you're sleeping with my sister, and then you're going to be the one getting angry?"

"It's just... It's a little bit too neat, don't you think? Fate brought our parents together and..." I shake my head.

"Sorry. I shouldn't say fate. Like it was meant to be. It wasn't meant to be that your mom died."

"I don't know why the things that happen happen," Gentry says. "Fate or otherwise. I have no insight. I don't know if there's a grand plan, divine design, or if everything is just desperately random. If a butterfly beats its wing next to a babbling brook that means we'll have six more weeks of winter, and someone you love will die. I don't know. What I do know is that life is random. Because it's difficult. Because it often sucks, when you get something good, you need to hang onto it with both hands. And I think my sister could be really good for you."

"Can I be really good for her?"

There's a long silence between the two of us. "I think that would depend on you."

"And I don't like that bet. She and I have already discussed it. She's got her life, her goals, I have mine. You can see why we wanted to keep it a secret. Because there's just no point. There's no point letting all this out. No point in having to make it the subject of gossip. Or family drama."

"I think you're making a mistake."

"Great," I say. "I'll make a note of that. But you think it's a mistake. But I think in the future, you won't feel that way. I think you'll feel exactly like I do. That it was for the best that she and I let each other grow. For what it's worth, being with her has made me better. I don't know what I've done for her. But she's made me think about things I never have. She's a pretty incredible woman."

"I know."

"There's a difference between it meaning nothing and it being forever."

"Great. Glad he filled me in."

"You're not changing your opinion, are you?"

"You've known me a long time. Have you ever known me to change an opinion?"

"I guess not."

"No. This is no exception."

"Don't say anything to her. She really didn't want anyone to know."

"Okay," Gentry says. "I won't."

I can tell he's mad at me. I can tell he's lost respect for me.

I expected that. And it's honestly more comfortable than him telling me I'm good. Than him telling me I do deserve her.

Because that just can't be true.

I don't have anything to offer her. That's the bottom line.

I'm a broken-up cowboy who doesn't know who he is outside the spotlight. I crashed out yesterday, but I might not have hit rock bottom yet.

I'm not dragging her down with me.

I didn't spend this many years trying not to be my dad only to fuck it up now.

Especially not with her.

She's not going to be some experiment. Not going to be my trial and error at a happy ending.

Not because she doesn't matter.

Because she matters too much.

Chapter Sixteen

Allison

Time just keeps rolling on relentlessly. It's almost September, Colt is doing physical therapy three days a week, and so close to getting off crutches it's borderline miraculous.

I've been going with him to the hospital for some of his in-person sessions. It is a long drive. I'm glad that I'm moving. I really am. I tell myself that every time I take that long ass trip to Tolowa. I have my apartment picked out, the deposit put down. I had money in savings from the job at Sammy's.

So I was able to do that on my own. The rent is higher than what I was paying at Cindy's place. The deal she was giving me was too good to be true.

My dad has offered to cover any expenses I can't cover on my own, and I'm grateful all over again for the support of my family.

I have so much. So the fact that I still feel the sort of hollow, unsatisfied feeling in my stomach as time ticks by is a me problem. I'm not missing anything. Not really.

Yes, I have strong feelings for Colt. Yes, I'm not looking forward to the physical aspect of our relationship ending – who would be excited about losing such great sex? No one I know. It's sex. That's all.

"I want to drive back." Colt says as we head out of the session.

"You're not tired?"

"I am tired. But I'm making progress. So... You've been driving me everywhere. I think I should get to take care of you too."

"I don't need it."

"Everyone needs it sometimes."

Not me. I don't want to need it. Because the minute you need someone, you could lose them. Better to be needed. It's why taking care of Colt has been so great. And yes, there's been a lot of sex, and I've enjoyed it, but I don't want... I don't want to get used to this. I don't want to get used to him caring for me.

But he doesn't listen, and he drives that long drive back.

"You know, I should make dinner."

He's made dinner a few times over these past months. But combined with what he said earlier, it makes me feel slightly uncomfortable. Still, he does it anyway, and I don't stop him. Because even though there is a reservation inside of me, part of me is hungry for it. It's honestly my whole experience with Colt. I know better, but I want it. I want it, so I let myself have it, I'm perilously close to the edge. Perilously close to falling off, falling to my death.

I know it, but I let him.

The best thing about today was that he got the all-clear

to take his brace off for things like bathing. He's still not supposed to put weight on it, or do anything else with the brace off, but he can do that.

"I think we should take a bath," he whispers.

"What?"

"I can officially get in water now." He grimaces. "I can't say that I love the look of my leg when that brace came off, though."

He's lost muscle, that's true. But it's also to be expected. I can see why it bothers him, though. But it doesn't bother me at all. It's just part of this. That feeling of edging ever closer to a precipice grows more profound. It's like when we had the picnic. He's teasing me with romanticism, and that's not supposed to be us.

I'm supposed to be able to sort all that out. I'm supposed to have gone into this with my eyes open. And yet I'm panicking.

I also still don't tell him no.

Instead, I enjoy our grilled corn salad and pork chop, because he really is a great cook, and then I let him go and run a bath. I sit there and act like the one who needs to be pampered. I let him, because there's been so little of this in my life, my choice.

I've dated men who let me baby them. I flung myself into this thing with Colt when he was in need of a caregiver. Because I know how to be a caregiver. I know how to make myself important.

And I always choose men that I... Can live without.

Always. Maybe I choose mediocre sex for that same reason. Nobody's crying over it ending in that case.

I'm suddenly sitting there in the kitchen looking at a long view of so many decisions that I've made. Deciding not to go to school and live on campus, deciding to depend on myself, take it at my own pace, do it online rather than building a whole network of friends and experiences apart from this place. And even now, now that I'm moving away, it isn't because I'm so excited to expand, it's because I wanted an excuse to distance Colt. Because I used it at the very beginning of all of this to draw a line in the sand, so that...

I gave it a diagnosis. A prognosis.

I made it so that it was something I could manage. So that it was fatal. Because if it were fatal, then I could just accept.

Because I know how to do that. I didn't want to be in a position where I was fighting. And fighting alone. To try and save this, to try and make it something it can never be.

He comes back into the room. "Ready."

I get up, and I go to him. I let him undress me in the bathroom, his rough hands skimming over my skin, making me sigh. I try to push all my thoughts away. All my doubts. The heaviness. The heavy feeling that I can't deny anymore.

It's never been a crush.

I love this man. I love this broken, fucked up man.

I have for a very long time.

And I never wanted it to be central to my life. I never wanted him to be central to my life because... He's made it so clear he doesn't want this.

I don't want this.

I don't want to be railing at the sky. I don't want to be begging for a miracle. One that I'm not going to get.

I just want to be able to live.

I've done this already. I've hoped for the impossible. I've prayed that I would be the exception. I don't want to do it again.

I fixed it all. I can accept it. I lost my mom, and it was terrible. But I can accept that it happened. I can turn it into something good. But going through the work of all that, it's a Herculean effort, and I just don't want to do it again, and here I am with this crushing weight, this awful, terrible feeling bearing down on me, and I just don't want to deal with it. I squeeze my eyes shut, and I let his hands take me away. I let this moment stand on its own.

"Someday. Someday, maybe I'll be able to pick you up." Except there is no someday, and we both know it. Our eyes connect, and I can feel the acknowledgment of that.

I just step into the tub, and I sit down. I expect him to join me, to slide in behind me, press his hard cock up against my ass. He doesn't. Instead, he undresses, and kneels down behind the tub.

And he starts washing my hair.

"Is your leg okay?"

"It is," he says. "Don't worry. I know how to make sure I don't hurt myself. It's been almost three months."

"Yeah," I say. "It has.

It's been three months. Three months since the accident. Three months since everything between us changed. Since his life changed. Since everything changed.

It's been three months.

And eventually it's going to fade away with time. Like all these things do. It'll be nothing but a blip on the radar of my life. And yet somehow I can't imagine it not feeling big. Not feeling significant. Not being this defining moment in my life.

I need it to not be. I need it to shrink away. But some things don't. No matter how big they are.

Just like a loss can still feel bigger than the sky after ten years. I think that the loss of this, the loss of him, will be my whole view for longer than I want.

But I let him wash my hair. Those big hands scrubbing my scalp, moving down over my breasts. That's when he finally decides to get in the water with me.

I let him. I let him fold me up into his arms, let our slick bodies slide together. I let him kiss me until we're both breathless.

Why does it feel like a goodbye? It's getting closer to one.

And that makes me want to die.

I've loved Colt Campbell since I was eleven years old. I'm afraid I'm going to love him forever.

This is being in love.

God. I'm in love.

It's not wonderful. It's painful and terrifying and horrendous.

And it's going to swallow me whole.

For a moment, I let it. I let him.

I let him kiss me all over the place, let the water make our skin slick, the slow glide of our bodies driving me wild.

He gets out, so do I. I'm a little surprised he didn't take me in the tub. But when he leads me to the bed, I get it. He grips my face and comes down over the top of me, kissing me hard as he thrusts deep inside of me. Now that he could do this without one leg off the bed. Without contorting. Without accommodating that brace, he's ready to take me like this. And he does. Hard. Fast. Every stroke a revelation.

It's like this every time. Like he's showing me new aspects of myself. Like he's healing and breaking me all at once.

When I cry out my climax, I know I'm going to break this. Because I can't accept it.

I can't accept it.

I don't just want to walk off into nothing. I don't just want a quiet end.

I want to fight.

Even if it kills me.

"Colt," I whisper. "I love you."

Chapter Seventeen

Colt

Her words are like a knife straight through my chest. Or maybe more accurately, a bullhorn.

She loves me? There's no way.

I can't accept it.

Because I'm not good for her. I know that. I know it.

And someday she's going to realize it. Someday she'll realize that I'm nothing.

The strange twist in my thinking almost takes my breath away. I'm not good enough, because I might hurt her. I'm not good enough, and she might hurt me.

Two different things. Not good enough because I'm a narcissist. Or just not good enough because there's something fundamentally wrong with me. My own dad doesn't love me. He never did.

Is it me? Is there something wrong with me? Something fundamentally broken.

So that I have to shine brighter, burn faster, try harder

than everybody else so that someone, anyone will love me. But I've inflicted myself on her, and that was never the idea.

"Allison... I think that's... We can't."

"I know," she says. "I know. For all the reasons we discussed. And I don't care. So what if everyone knows? Let's just let them know."

"We can't," I say. "You know how everyone in town will react, and mom and your dad..."

"I don't care. What if I don't care? What if I feel like this is worth more than any of that? What if I feel like it's more important for us to fight for this, to fight for each other, than it is to worry at all what anyone else thinks? We'll deal with them later. Let's deal with us first."

"There's nothing to deal with. I need to get back to the rodeo."

"I thought you were going to... Deal with that. I thought you were going to get some therapy."

"I am. I will. But God, I can't go dragging you into all this."

"Don't I get a choice?"

"You had a choice," I say. "From the beginning, you had a choice. I told you exactly what was going to happen. You agreed to it."

She sits up, pulling her knees up to her chest. "Okay. But I want to change it."

"No. I can't."

It's the fear that's roaring through me that I don't understand. The abject terror. It's like there's a wind tunnel in my ears, and all I can hear is the screaming, deafening noise.

She loves me. But for how long? Why? It doesn't make any sense to me. It doesn't make any sense.

And the truth is, I can't really believe it. Not in any

lasting sense. Because it just doesn't make sense to me. It doesn't. It can't.

Because I can't.

I can't be what she wants I can't... My thoughts are a blur. I can't say that I feel like I'm making much sense even in my own head. All I know. All I can even latch onto is the fear.

I'm letting it drive me. I'm letting it push me.

"I want us to still have what we can. I want us to still do what we talked about. To have this not... Ruin anything."

"It's too late. The thing is, Colt, I love you. And I have loved you. I've loved you since I was eleven. And I can't pretend that I don't. I can't pretend that I didn't. I'm not just going to accept half because you're afraid."

She stares at me. "That's it, isn't it? You're scared that I'm going to leave you. Because when is it going to be good enough? Do you think that you're going to win the championship and then never feel shady about yourself ever again? Because I don't think so. I don't think that's what's going to happen, and you're lying to yourself. That there's going to be some benchmark. You were close when you said that you needed therapy. But I don't think it's so you can be different than your dad. I think you need therapy so you can accept that nothing you do is ever going to make him love you. Nothing. And even if you did something that was so great it made him look at you, then what? Is that love?"

She lets out a hard, sharp breath. "That's what you do, all around town, isn't it? You have to be the golden boy. You have to be him or you don't know who you are or what you are. So the idea of me just loving you while you're like this freaks you out. Because you don't know what to do with that. You don't know how to earn it. You don't know how to make yourself good enough for it. Do you think you're just going to push me away so that I can't do it to you? Because that's what you're afraid of."

Her words cut me deep. And I'm waiting for the measured Allison to show up. The one that talked so philosophically about life and loss.

But she's not being philosophical about this. She's not being measured. Her eyes are glittering with angry tears, and she's looking at me like I'm a coward. But I guess I am.

"I'm not rejecting you," I say. "It's just that–"

"Do you love me or not?"

"I can't do this with you right now."

"Do you love me or not?"

"Allison..."

"Not. In which case, you are rejecting me."

"You're the one who changed things. It can still –"

"I'm not taking half," she screams. "I'm not taking half. I want everything. God dammit. Why don't I get to have everything? I want ecstatic love and sex and to be happy. I'm tired of just accepting that life is hard. I'm so fucking tired of hard. Great. Life can be this goddamn constant struggle. Where you just put your head down and you try to take all the bad things with grace, and I've done that. But I'm over it. When you want everything, when you want to stop just carrying it all on your shoulders, let me know. Until then, I'm glad that you made enough progress to take the brace off sometimes. I'm glad that you're healing. What I really hope is that someday you find the thing. The magic thing, that makes Colt Campbell good enough. I'm betting you won't find it though. Somehow. I just bet."

And then she storms out of the bedroom naked. I lay there, and I'm surprised when this pinprick of sensation in my chest becomes a deep, relentless stab. Worse than anything I've ever felt. Worse than any physical pain.

I don't know what I just did.

Beyond screwup maybe the best thing that's ever happened to me. I see myself again, as a little kid. My life flashing before my eyes, just like I'm bleeding out in the arena. Dying, this time without an audience.

Did you see me?

She does see me. She does.

I spent my whole life chasing the approval of a man who didn't, who wouldn't, who won't.

And ran away from the only woman who ever did.

Chapter Eighteen

Allison

I don't go home. Instead, I go to Sarah's. And as soon as she opens the door, I burst into tears.

"Oh no," she says. "Come in."

"Is Dallas home?" I ask.

"He had to go to his parents for something. He'll be back soon, though."

"I just... I don't want to..."

"It's Colt, isn't it?"

I look at her helplessly. "We both know, Allison. Don't worry about it. We figured it out."

"But I..."

I don't even have the energy to defend myself. To defend us.

"Why didn't you say anything?"

"Because. I figured if you wanted me to know you would've told me. I figured that it was probably kind of complicated. I wanted to let it be complicated, and let you talk about it when you needed to. And look, I was right. You need to now."

"That's... Really... Nonjudgmental of you."

"I haven't had a lot of friends in my life, and I admit, I didn't know if this was something I should actually be pushing about. Something that I should've tried to get you to share, but I didn't want to push you too hard. And if there's one thing I know, being a kid with a certain amount of trauma and getting bounced around to different places, I always felt safer with the people who waited for me to tell them what I needed, or what was wrong. Rather than the people who pushed me when I wasn't ready."

"Well, thank you. I should've trusted you from the beginning, I feel. But it was just... I thought that we would just do it for a while, and then we would stop, and it would be fine. But I love him."

Sarah wraps her arms around me. "I know. I know you do. And it feels really miserable."

"Yes." I bury my head in my hands. "I think I went too far. I demanded things from him that he's not ready to give."

"Well, love's weird. And intense. So if you're a little weird and intense while you're experiencing it, that feels fair."

"But I might've just blown everything up."

"Well, now he has to figure out what he's going to do."

"He's scared. He doesn't know who he is when he's not winning. And he's turned it into this whole thing about how him chasing the spotlight means he's like his dad, but that's not it. He's just scared that if the spotlight's not on him, no one will want him. And maybe I could've been gentler, maybe I could've accepted where he was at more but I'm just... I'm tired. I'm tired of being measured and accepting. I just wanted..."

"You're tired of taking care of other people. You're tired of not depending on people. Believe me, I get that. I had to kind of be my own little island for a really long time. And when I was done, I was done. You don't have to apologize for that."

"But I might've ruined everything." Or," she says. "You might've fixed it."

I keep thinking about the conversation I had with him a little while ago. About how this had happened to him, so he could find other healing. And I cling to that as I cry on Sarah's couch. The idea that this has to happen for there to be real healing. For there to be a real resolution. That I had to take it there in order to fix it. That might just be wishful thinking, and that's not something I usually do.

But I need it now. I need it because after everything I've been through, this is the thing that might actually break me.

It's like somehow I always knew.

That he would be the one to shatter me entirely.

But even as I weep, I find myself filled with a strange sort of strength and gratitude.

Because I don't know that it was ever clearer to me the way that I've lived safely, the way that I've held back, until now.

And I'm not going to do that anymore.

I might feel broken, but I'm not. I'm stronger than I've ever been. I know exactly who I am. I know exactly what I want.

"No guts, no glory," I whisper.

I might not have the glory, but God damn, I have guts.

I know that now.

And it's something I'm going to carry with me for the rest of my life. Even if I can't have him.

Chapter Nineteen

Colt

It's been a month since Allison told me she loved me.

It's been a month of hell.

I've barely seen her. She moved. I didn't go help.

Nobody made a big deal out of it, because they all assumed it had to do with my injury. Except Gentry, who came by and had a conversation with me that was filled with thinly veiled threats.

Allison hasn't said anything to him, I know that much. But it doesn't mean he hasn't picked up on the vibe.

Dallas and Sarah know, and I can feel Sarah's disappointment every time I'm near her. Dallas has known me for too long to turn on me like that. It isn't like Sarah has *totally* turned on me, and in fact, we've decided to go to the bull riding championships in Vegas together.

I'm not sure that I should go. I don't know if it's going to push me over the edge or not. But it's something I feel compelled to do. Like I have to sit there and watch this thing get taken away from me so that I can really...

I want to be able to win still. I want pretty damned badly.

"You didn't have to come," Dallas says as we take our seats.

"I did," I say. Though I don't expand on it. I just know that I had to.

I don't really know why. Maverick is in the final, so even though it's not as personal for Dallas, he is kind of hate watching. We just all hate that guy.

We've got great seats, and when I look down toward the walkway, I see a familiar face.

"It's Stella," I say.

I'm surprised to see Stella at an exclusively bull-riding event. Especially since neither Dallas nor I is in the final. Which is maybe... I don't know, a little bit egotistical. But still. Barrel racing is her thing, and we are her best friends outside of that.

Sarah stands up and immediately starts waving. She only met Stella once, as far as I'm aware. But of course she recognizes her. Stella is pretty memorable. A tough-as-nails rodeo rider. If she had been a man, and the path had been clear to be a bull rider, she would've been a damn good one.

She makes a beeline toward where we are in the stands. She walks a couple of steps up, and stands next to the empty chair beside us. It will be filled soon. The event is sold out. But we are early, and everyone is still milling around.

"You guys have no idea how weird it is to not have you haunting me all year."

Dallas stands and gives her a hug. I stand too, even if a little more slowly. I'm totally off crutches now, doing well, but I'm definitely experiencing effects. I can feel the weather in my bones, and I can't say I had that skill before.

But I feel like the outlook is good.

At least for my body.

The outlook for my heart is another matter.

My fault. I know it is. My fault that I screwed things up with her. That I couldn't say yes. I feel like I proved everything that I always believed about myself. Going back to her wouldn't even be doing her a favor.

"You look rough, buddy," Stella says, coming in for a hug. "I love you anyway, though."

"Thanks."

"I didn't expect you here."

"I didn't expect you here," I say.

Her face goes red. I know I didn't imagine it.

"Oh," I say. "You're here with someone. Or for someone."

She clears her throat. "Not really."

"I don't believe that," Dallas says.

Sarah is looking between us, keen.

"Are you on a date with Alexandra Bella?" She's the reigning rodeo queen, and I've never been able to get a read on Stella's preferences, so it's as logical as anything else.

She laughs. "I almost wish, Colt. She seems like a good time."

"So the person you're with is not a good time," Sarah asks.

"I'm by myself," she responds.

"Here to see one of the guys ride?"

"You know," she lifts her nose in the air, "I don't really care who wins. And there is a likelihood someone could have a terrible accident, just like you."

There's bitterness underlying her tone. I recognize it because I'm pretty damn sure I did that to Allison.

"Is it Maverick Quinn?" Sarah asks, and we all turn to look at her.

"*No*," Dallas and I say at the same time.

"He sucks," I say.

"He really does," Dallas agrees.

She doesn't say anything in response, and my stomach turns with relative horror. I pinch the bridge of my nose. "Oh God, Stella."

Dallas shoves his hands in his pockets.

"People who live in glass houses shouldn't throw stones," Sarah says, looking at Colt.

"Excuse me? What did I do?"

"You know what you did," she says.

"I... Wow, Sarah."

"Whatever," Stella says. I shouldn't have even come. He got me tickets when he qualified. But then things were different. Or maybe, things were... I don't know." Her eyes filled with tears. She blinks them away, and it's awful, looking at this. This kind of heartbreak. Because I feel it. Deep down inside of myself. Stella is a wonderful woman, and he's not worth shit. That much is clear. He's a jerk, he's older than we are, unfriendly to absolutely everybody. Arrogant. He's like me, but if I chose to use my powers for evil rather than good. He has dark charisma. That's undeniable. But I thought that Stella knew better than to get tangled up with somebody like him. I guess that's the problem.

When you want somebody, you don't know better. You deliberately decide not to know better.

I think that's what Allison did with me. I can't say that I've done much better for myself. I wanted what I wanted, even though I couldn't follow through.

"Any guy who fumbles you is an idiot," Sarah says decisively.

Stella snorts. "I think I'm the idiot. For getting overly involved with a man who stated up front that he was going to fumble me. Without getting into the details."

"I'm here for details," says Sarah.

Dallas and I look at each other.

I don't really want to think about Stella getting hot and heavy with Maverick Quinn. I hate that guy. Also, she's actually like a sister to me. In a way, Allison certainly never was.

I went and made my life way too complicated. Why are feelings complicated?

I growl at that internal thought. Because they are. And I don't like them. They just hurt.

I've had enough pain. A whole gut full of it.

Stella and Sarah are whispering, and pretty soon it's time for Stella to go find her seat.

"I have a seat in the box," Stella says. "Motherfucker couldn't take those tickets back. Just everything else. See you guys later."

She leaves, a hard edge to her defiant smile. It's very her that she's here no matter what.

I never saw Stella have a relationship, not in all the years I knew her on the circuit.

"This is what happens when we leave," I say. "She makes bad decisions."

Both Dallas and Sarah look at me. "What?"

"It could be argued that you are also the architect of some supremely bad decisions," Dallas says.

"I didn't ask you."

"I didn't wait to be asked."

"Y'all are some assholes," I growl.

"You kind of deserve it," Sarah says. "We're your friends. And we love you. We do. We love you. But loving you means also being realistic about the fact that you really messed up with Allison."

"I did it for her."

"You did it for you, Bud," Dallas says. "Because you're scared. And I get that. Believe me. We've all been through it."

"I just... I wanted to do better. To be better. Before... I don't know. I feel like I've proven that I can't be."

"Fatalistic nonsense," Sarah says.

I grit my teeth, and then it's time for the event to start. There is so much spectacle involved in the world championship. It's here in Vegas, after all. There's a big country star singing the anthem, and trick riders who come out in the beginning. The production values are high. I've been lucky enough to participate in a number of years. It's great. A rush like nothing else. Sitting here, watching it, is an interesting form of self-flagellation that I've chosen.

But, I feel like I deserve it.

The rides are incredible. There's not a single man here who doesn't deserve it. The animals are in peak condition. I didn't know how I would feel, actually watching this again. Being near the animals like this. But the surge in my heart tells me that I can heal from this. I can go back to it. My body will let me. Maybe I won't ever be able to be the best.

But I do love this.

Maybe I won't ever be the best.

That whispers through me, and it feels like terror. Like I might have actually just been told the time of my own death.

Maybe I won't ever be the best.

And then what? What will anything mean? Why will I have done any of it?

Why did I push her away?

Because then she'll push me away. When I can't be everything.

Finally, it's time for Maverick Quinn to ride.

"He's going to win," Dallas says in my ear. "The son of a bitch is going to win."

We both knew it. From the beginning, we both knew that without us, it was going to be him. Not that he couldn't beat us. So much of it has to do with the luck of the draw. What the animal is doing. So much of it has to do with circumstances you can't control.

It's an interesting thing that I've chosen as my profession. Given that I sure as hell try to control everything else. And everyone's reactions to me. Maybe that's why I'm good at bull riding, actually. Because I'm always doing a dance. Always balancing. Contorting and twisting and putting on the best show possible.

When Maverick is released from the shoot, it's like there's a breath held for a moment in the whole stadium. Just for a second. Because from the beginning, you can tell that it's a special ride. That everything is going his way. The bull is putting up a fight, but Maverick is dominating. Everything is working exactly like it has to. It's a winning ride.

"He is winning," I say.

"Motherfucker," says Dallas.

"Oh boy," says Sarah. "Stella is going to need emotional support after."

Eight seconds. He makes it. He leaps off the bull, and I'm used to him turning away from the crowd. Instead, he turns toward the box. Stella isn't there. I watch as a man that I've never seen show a speck of emotion beyond anything bad, looks... Lost. That's what he looks like. Lost.

He just won. I know he did. His score is going to come up any moment, and it's going to show that he is the world champion.

He just got everything. Everything I've ever wanted. And he...

He's not happy.

I watch him, and I don't feel envy. That blows me away. Because I would've told you that I would feel nothing but an intense stab of envy for the man who won this. This thing that I've always believed was going to make me feel whole.

But I can see that he doesn't. I can see that he's not. Then they show his score. He's the clear winner. One million. Bragging rights. An undisputed champion. One of the few to be declared the best. He is walking like a man who thinks he's the best.

In fact, he walks right out of the arena. Yes, there will be a ceremony later, and yes, it just so happens he was the last ride and the top score, and he'll probably come back but... It was the perfect opportunity. For a victory lap. To gloat. To bask in the fact that he is the very best. The very best.

And yet it doesn't seem to have changed anything for them. Because his arms are empty.

Because whatever he had with Stella, he messed it up.

All that could be you. Yeah. It could be. Me. Basking in that glory, with absolutely nothing.

It didn't make him good. It won't make me good either.

With a horrible, hollow feeling in my stomach, I realize how right Sarah and Dallas are about me.

I really thought all this time it was going to fix something that was broken. Prove something that I'm not sure can be proven.

That I'm good. That I matter. That my dad made a mistake abandoning me. And I can't believe that lives so deep inside of me, because I know that man is a narcissist. I do. But everything is twisted up inside of me. The shrapnel of a broken childhood. Trying to figure out whether I'm wrong or he's wrong, or if it's a little bit of both.

I stand up, and I walk silently away from the spectacle, heading toward the corridor, which is still mostly empty. I stand there, feeling like my legs are about to collapse underneath me. It wouldn't really be a shock, considering the one leg is still problematic.

"What's up?"

I turn and see Dallas standing behind me. My closest friend. The person who maybe knows me the most of anyone. Except for Allison.

"This didn't fix him," I say. "He won, I've never seen anybody look so broken."

"You're feeling empathy for Maverick? This is a weird day."

"Yeah. Because that would be me, wouldn't it? I'd win, it wouldn't matter. I'd win, but it wouldn't fix anything. I'd win, and I still wouldn't... I wouldn't have her."

"Yeah, Colt, that's about the size of it."

"But I needed to fix myself. I needed to make myself feel like I was good enough."

Dallas clears his throat and moves toward me. "Nothing is going to do that. And I get that it doesn't mean a lot coming from a guy who already won, because I guess it's easy for me to say. But if you can't be okay with who you are without all of that, you're never going to be okay with it. Sarah is what makes it feel like I'm okay. Sarah is the one thing that makes me feel like I am right where I need to be, all the time."

"My mom is a good mom, and she loves me. My stepdad is great. I've got good friends."

"It doesn't mean you don't have wounds. I have the best family. And still, there was just something that felt like it was missing inside of me. Something broken. She's the one who fixed it. It's not your body she was helping heal all this time, Colt. It was your soul. But you have to let it. You can't be good enough unless you decide that you are. And if you can't believe that, then look at yourself the way that she does. You know she never liked you because of that golden boy stuff. She just sees you. I think more people do than you realize. What would happen if you stepped off the stage? What would happen if you just lived?"

What would happen? If I just lived. I don't even know. I don't know what to do with this feeling of not being worthy of it that still rolls around inside of me. I don't know what to do with all of this. But I know that I miss Allison. I know everything in my life has been worse since she left, that even as my body has healed, my heart has felt damaged. I know that.

And I need her. But I don't know what I offer her. I just... She's the most generous, beautiful, wonderful woman I've ever known. She calls me out, she makes me feel like I have a home. I'm always running, and with her, I don't want to do that.

But then I think about the way she fought for us. Fought for me. The way that she saw me.

Yeah, the idea of her turning away from me fills me with dread. But if I don't try, that's what makes me my dad. Except worse. He can't care about other people. I can. If I know better, and I don't choose to do better, but I'm really not better than he is.

I can have a happier life. I just have to choose to be brave. Ironic for someone who does my job. But that's not real bravery. Real bravery is being afraid and doing it.

And the real value of a man, I think, is his ability to do that. I haven't been.

So I have to pick myself back up, and I have to try to make myself someone she deserves. I'm not there yet.

But what I can do is something my father never did. Try.

"I need to go fix something."

"Yeah, you do," Dallas says. "It's about time."

"Healing is a process," I say. "And it takes longer than I'd like."

But at least I've decided that I'm going to do it. At least.

Chapter Twenty

Allison

The night of the championship, Sarah sends me a petty text about the fact that Colt's nemesis won the championship. But I don't even feel gratified by that. I'm tired from a long shift at the hospital, and I'm waiting still for everything to get better. My heartbreak. Missing him.

It just isn't.

I've been avoiding coming to family dinners. The fallout is exactly what I was afraid of.

It didn't just affect my relationship with him.

It's affecting my relationship with everyone.

But this is heartbreak, deep and real, and even though I know I'm going to be okay, even though I know my life has purpose outside of this man, it doesn't make the pain just stop. It's the strangest feeling. Because in many ways, I feel stronger. More certain of myself. Otherwise, I just feel... Gross.

I'm also surprised when there's a knock on my apartment door at 10:30 at night, and I practically dive under my couch cushions with my phone, ready to call 911.

Then I hear his voice through the door.

"Allison? Please open the door."

Colt.

I get up, my heart in my throat as I run to open it. "What the hell are you doing here? You gave me a heart attack. Is everyone okay? Gentry?"

My brother is always out doing something dangerous, and my first thought is for him and his safety.

"No," he says. "I'm sorry. I should've called you. I should've texted you. But after the championship last night, I was just focused on getting home as quickly as I could."

"Did you drive?"

"I did. I had to get back. I had to get to you."

"I know that guy you hate won."

Colt nods. "Yeah. He did. And I didn't really care that much. You know what, neither did he. I watched him win, and I watched it be hollow.

He's the same asshole.

The same asshole that I've always thought he was. Just a winner."

He looks haunted, hunted. Sad. "It doesn't change you," he continues. "I know that stuff, I do. But somewhere deep inside of myself, I was counting on a magic potion. To fix me. To make me feel like enough. I decided that it was the rodeo. I decided it was the championship. Because that's where my dad was. And it was like everything in my life had to go on hold until I won that. Until I proved that I was worth something. Then I fucked my leg up, and everything got twisted and bent out of shape, including me. It felt like being with you was..."

He sighs. "I don't know, like maybe I could, but not

until I prove that I was worthy. But I'm never going to feel worthy. Ever. That's... Childhood trauma for you, I guess. So I just have to beg you to be okay with me. I'm not perfect. Hell, I'm so far from it I... I screwed everything up with you. Absolutely everything. I hurt you, I... God, Allison. I am so sorry for everything that I did. Everything I didn't do. All of my own stuff that I projected onto you. It was wrong."

I feel like I'm going to break apart, and I can tell that he is too. His hands are shaking. His whole body is shaking.

"Colt," I whisper. I reach out, and I put my hand on his face. "You really hurt me."

"I know."

"But you're not dead."

"What does that mean?" He looks at me, mystified.

"It means that there's always a chance. I told you that I wanted to fight. I meant that. I mean it. Right now. I want to fight for us. For this. Because I love you. Because I know what it's like to just have to accept when something can't make it, but we can. I love you. And I can forgive you. For hurting me. For breaking us up. Because you're here. You don't need to be good enough for me. You don't need to be a golden boy. You don't need to be anything. Not anything except you. You forget, I've known you since we were kids. I've known a lot of versions of you."

He steps forward, takes my hand and presses it to his chest. "I'm sorry that I made us wait this long. I'm sorry that it took me a month to get my shit together."

I'm glad it did, honestly. Now, standing there, staring at him, my shattered heart slowly knitting itself back together in my chest, I'm glad it happened. We faced the worst thing between us, so we can face everything else. Everyone else.

All the fallout – whatever that will look like. The shift in our family dynamic, in our lives.

I'm going to start a new career. He's going to...we don't know yet.

Now we know how much we can handle. And I know he'll choose me because he did it now. He stared down what scared him most, and he chose to come back to me. To risk himself emotionally.

I'm glad he took the time, even though it hurt, because it's why I know my answer now, too.

"It's okay. It's okay that it did. Because we're going to have forever, aren't we?"

"We *are* going to have forever, and a whole town full of people talking about us."

"I don't mind that. I really don't. Because you and I, we don't need to please anyone else. Only us."

It's like a burden has been lifted off of him, I can see it. And I really see him for the first time. This man, who has spent his whole life trying to be worthy of the accolades he's gotten, of the way that people feel about him.

"You know, I just loved you. The whole time. Before you ever made something of yourself. Before you were ever any kind of champion. And I will always love you. Because with us, cowboy, it's always a perfect ride."

He bends down and picks me up, and I gasp. Because the whole time, he hasn't been able to do this. We've never been able to do this. "Oh," I say.

"God, I've been wanting to do this forever," he says. "And I just... I love you, Allison. I love you. I've always thought that in life, if you didn't have guts, you couldn't have glory. But I've been brave about the wrong things. This... This is the bravest thing two people can do. Just love each other."

I smile, because he's right. The world is scary and dangerous. It's filled with dark and terrible things. But it's filled with light and hope, and the extraordinary passion that two people can feel for each other. It's a gift. I'm so glad that we both get to grab onto it with everything we are. I'm so grateful that I didn't just accept anything. I'm so grateful I fought for him. For us.

I lean in and kiss him on the mouth. "You're good enough just the way you are."

Chapter Twenty-One

Colt

We tore the apartment up last night.

Part of my apology tour, which I don't think is going to be over anytime soon.

Not because she's holding anything against me. No. She told me she loved me last night more times than I can count, and I made sure to say it two times to her every one, because I owe her.

"What exactly do you want to do?" I ask while lying in her bed, staring at the unfamiliar ceiling. "We can long distance. If that makes you more comfortable. I know you're doing school, and I'm not doing much of anything but lying around, then healing myself."

She props herself up on her elbow and looks at me. "Is that what you want to do?"

I turn toward her. "Hell no. I want to move in with you. Or to have you move in with me. But I'm the one who messed up."

"You're not on probation," she says, leaning in and kissing me on the nose. Which is far too sweet given the circumstances. She sits up.

"I'm going to need you to forgive yourself, because your self-loathing is actually the problem. You made a mistake. That's all. It's not a mistake that comes from nothing."

I sit with that for a moment. "I'm just really sorry that I hurt you."

"I know. Do you think your dad has ever been sorry about hurting anyone? Do you think he's ever worried so much about being a good person?"

"No," I say, a little bit dumbfounded by that realization. But of course it's true. Of course, he's never worried about that.

"Your love is good enough." I duck my head, suddenly overwhelmed by emotion. I let out a hard breath, and look at her. I let her see it. I've gone through all this and not shed a single tear, but she makes me want to weep like a baby. Because what she said is true. She's loved me forever. Even when she was kind of a brat to me, she loved me. What a difficult position she was in, all these years. Feeling like it was impossible. She's brave enough to have taken a chance on us years ago, but the connection...

We still have to deal with our respective parents. With the way this is going to affect the family. But that feels extremely secondary to us knowing we've made a real commitment to each other.

"I would like to live here," she says finally. "Just because I'm not sure how I feel about us cohabitating in a house your mom owns."

"We've had more sex in houses owned by my mom than can be readily catalogued."

She laughs. "I know. But for our life. If you don't mind."

"I don't mind. I've traveled all over the place. I can do apartment living for a little bit."

She wraps her arms around mine. "You're still a cowboy, you know."

Something about that goes a long way to healing a sore spot in my chest. "I want to go talk to your dad."

I feel some real dread about that.

Because Jim is my father figure. Hell, he's just my dad. In ways my own certainly never has been. Robert Campbell doesn't care about me. He didn't send me anything when I got injured – the cascade of cards and texts that I received in the hospital didn't have a single thing to do with him. My hero in so many ways. A real man. Who bakes pies for his family, and loves his kids. Who went through something impossible, a grief that must've split him open. A grief I feel closer to now, now that I know what it's like to love somebody. Like this.

I don't want to do anything to compromise my relationship with him, and yet, Allison is the one thing that's worth it.

"I should probably talk to your mom."

"I can handle all that."

She shakes her head. "Divide and conquer. I think that seems fair."

"I assume Gentry has already talked to you," I say.

She wrinkles her nose. "No."

"Well. He knows. "He's a real friend. A *good* friend. I didn't appreciate what he was offering to me because it was something that disrupted my narrative. I appreciate it now, though. I really do.

I make breakfast, then we decide to make the trip to Golden Valley. It's a mirror, in many ways of that time she drove me home from the hospital. Except this time I'm healed. My body might not be totally healed, but my soul is. That matters a hell of a lot more. I never thought I'd be in that position, where what was inside me mattered more. Because all I wanted was to be able to win that championship. To prove myself. I don't have to do that anymore.

But as we pull up to the house, I do feel some fear. Those old feelings of insufficiency wash through me. Because patterns are hard to break.

As I get out of the driver's seat, Jim comes walking up from the direction of the barn. "What are you two doing here?"

"I want to talk to you," I say.

Allison doesn't touch me, but she does smile at me. "I'm going to go talk to Cindy," she says.

She walks away from the truck, up the stairs toward the house. I take a deep breath, and turn toward Jim. "I don't really know how to say this. So... I just have to." I close my eyes. "I love Allison."

I'm waiting for something. For an ax to fall, for a punch to get thrown. But he's just standing there, looking at me, and suddenly it seems absurd that I would think my gentle, lovely stepfather would suddenly throw a punch when he's never done any such thing. I realize how much of this comes from inside me. How much of it never had anything to do with him. All my insecurities, for all my life. They're just about me. I projected that mirror onto other people.

"Do you want to clarify, because there are a few ways I could take that."

I nod. "Yeah, I... I want to marry her. And I get that that's weird. Or maybe it feels like it's coming from nowhere. Or like it's not right, and I struggled with that a lot. We did."

Jim nods and lets out a long sigh. "Colt, you're not as

subtle as you think you are." He closes the distance between us and claps me on the shoulder. "It's been months of the two of you circling each other, being together, being distant, and when we moved Allison into her apartment and you weren't there, it was clear something had happened."

"You never treated me any differently."

"Neither of you were ready to talk about it. Cindy and I have talked about it. A lot. And we've been worried, but you can't drag things out of your kids when they're not ready to tell you."

God, I really am so lucky. There have been some unlucky things. But not this. My family... I'm so lucky there. "You're right. It's complicated," Jim said. "But in some ways, it doesn't surprise me. I know she had a crush on you when she was a kid. Again, not as subtle as she probably would've liked. I know she wasn't happy when Cindy and I got married. I thought it was about her mom, but I think it was a lot about you. You two have your own relationship. Just like Cindy and I have our own relationship. But you and I have our own relationship, Colt. And you will always be a son to me, no matter what. So when things weren't good with the two of you, you were still my son."

It's that unconditional love. That love I still never expect. That love, I don't know how to accept. But I'm trying. I'm learning. Because the inability to accept love is almost as bad as the inability to give it.

"Thanks," I say. "I needed that. More than you can imagine. I... I really do love her. And I'm going to take care of her. And I'm not going to ask her to marry me right away, because I know she's doing school, and I want her to feel like I've given all this thought, but..."

"Tell her you want to marry her," Jim says. "One thing I

can tell you for sure is that honesty is always the best thing. And also, don't let time get away from you."

He's speaking with authority, as a man who has deeply loved twice. Who understands what a gift it is. And I realize that what a gift that is to me. Because if anybody was going to be accepting, and not judge, it's someone who understands the weight and value of these feelings. "I have something for you. Why don't you come inside?"

"What?"

"I have her mom's ring. I've saved it. I want you to have it. So that you can give it to her."

I really am an emotional wreck today. But if something was going to wreck me, I think it's right that it's this. "I'd love that."

He puts his hand on my back, and we walk up the stairs into the house.

Allison and my mom are in the kitchen, and they walk through to us when we come in. My mom has tears in her eyes, and she hugs me. Tight. "I love you. I'm glad you're happy."

We stay for most of the afternoon, and the ring is burning a hole in my pocket. I was going to wait. But I don't want to wait. Because I almost died. And it's not missing the championship that would've been a tragedy. It's not missing guts and glory or anything else. It would be missing this.

And so instead of driving back to the apartment, I start to head up toward Medicine Lake.

"What are we doing?"

"Something really important," I say.

I parked the truck, and hold her hand as we walked to that same patch of grass where we made love and things changed between us. They really changed. This place knows us. It knows who we are and how deeply we feel for each other. And it feels right to get down on one knee right there in the grass. Here's where I told her that if she got pregnant I'd take care of her. It was the deepest offer I could make at the time. This is better.

"Allison, will you marry me?"

She looks stunned. "Colt, we..."

"We've already been together for a lifetime, in one form or another. I'm ready to step into the next lifetime. We can wait and get married after you're done with school. Or we can get married tomorrow. Whatever you want, but –"

She doesn't wait for me to finish. She wraps her arms around my neck and comes down to the ground with me, kissing me hard. I pull the ring out of my pocket and show her. "Your dad gave it to me."

Tears are streaming down her face. And she puts the ring on her finger, looking down at it. "Oh, I remember this. I remember this ring on my mom's hand."

"They've all given us their blessing."

She nods. "You know, I thought it was a mistake. When our parents first got married. Because I thought that I was supposed to be with you, and this was going to keep us away from each other. It wasn't a mistake. But sometimes life is tricky, and difficult things happen. Like me losing my mom. But there's beauty in it, and there's still a path to joy. And I'd like to think that in some way, all these shattered pieces worked together to bring us this moment, the whole diamond."

"I think so," I say. Because it was the same with me. I had to be broken, really broken, before I could be put back together. And now here I am, no crowd, no stage. And I've never been happier.

Epilogue

Colt

It took two years for me to get back on the circuit.

Two long years for me to get back to the championships. But it's funny, because I don't need it anymore. It's a strange thought, one that hits me hard just before I exit the chute.

I don't *need* this. It would be nice. Hell, I'd love to have the money. To take care of Allison. To pay for a really amazing wedding. Get us set up for life. Go on a honey-moon. But it's all about how it fits into my life now. It's not my life anymore. After this, win or lose, I'm done. Because I'm ready to start forever with her.

We have been the talk of the town. That much is true. We've been debated, discussed, gossiped about.

Now, nobody really blinks.

Because we're more a couple to everybody than we are stepsiblings. When we slipped into that new version of our lives, I realized how much that was always true.

What a funny thing to think about right before what *should* be the most critical eight seconds of my life.

But it's not.

Because there was the eight seconds before I kissed Allison for the first time. The eight seconds right when she climaxed with me for the first time and called out my name. That eight seconds where she looked up at me when I told her I loved her and asked me to forgive her, and I waited for her to respond.

The eight seconds it took to get a yes when I asked her to marry me.

Yeah. There are so many more intervals of eight seconds that matter far and away beyond this.

This is just another Friday night.

"Okay," I say to the bull underneath me, patting him on the shoulders. "Let's go, buddy."

The chute opens, and it's not unlike the championship ride I watched Maverick Quinn have a couple of years ago.

I just *know*.

I complete it, and it's perfect.

I've had the best season of my career. No one can take that from me, whatever the result. And how I feel about myself has nothing to do with this.

There are four riders after me, and I have to wait for their event scores to know exactly what all this means. To know if I finally win or not.

When all the scores are posted, I'm the clear winner. No one has managed to overtake me.

The chaos is incredible. People are running out onto the arena. I'm a comeback story. The biggest one for decades.

A man who nearly died in the arena two and a half years ago, now the champion of it.

Robert Campbell's son, who did what his father could

never do. And whether I want it to be or not, his legacy is linked to mine in this moment.

I knew he was here tonight, but that's not news. He's usually at these things.

What does shock me is when I look up, and I see Robert Campbell walking toward me. He makes eye contact with me. And I know he sees me.

He sticks out his hand. "You did well, son."

The thing is, his words don't change anything. They don't mean anything. That'll make me feel a lick of difference about myself.

I'm better than him. I succeeded. I won that the one thing he couldn't. He was a legend. A favorite, but never the winner.

And I am.

But it just doesn't matter.

Because I'm not him, I stick my hand out and shake his. "Thanks."

He opens his mouth like he expects us to have a conversation, a reckoning, a come-to-Jesus. But I'm already turning away from him. I don't see him. Because Allison is right there, lit up with joy and love. My mom is there. Gentry, Dallas.

My stepdad.

The man who treats me like a son in all the ways that matter. This is a moment of absolute triumph, but not for the reasons I imagined.

The truth is this: if there's no love, there's no glory.

I've had that glory all along.

Now, I know it.

Also by Maisey Yates

The Bull Riders

Colt

Maverick

Standalones

Happy After All

The First Witches Club

Short and Sweet

The Cowboy's Mail Order Bride - Historical western written as Millie Adams

Imagine Me and You

Her Little White Lie

Crazy, Stupid Sex

Lessons in Dominance (Multi-Author Series)

Rustler Mountain

Rustler Mountain

Outlaw Lake

Lonesome Ridge